"What's your hurry?" Lex asked, studying her.

Blond, slender, almost luminous, there was about Keely a bit of that smooth elegance the women in Chilton always had, the result of salon pampering, expensive cosmetics, luxurious clothing. Amazing what money could buy.

And yet… Though she was thinner and somehow even more brittle than he remembered, she was more beautiful than ever.

Keely Stafford. His brother's fiancée.

"Well, I'll be damned," he said.

Lex had known her as a kid, but she was all grown up. If she'd disturbed him then, he had a pretty good feeling she could send him right around the bend now. And besides her obvious attractions, there was something about her—a combination that caught a man's imagination…a combination that might make a man do anything to try to unlock the secret.

Even steal millions, if he had to.

Dear Reader,

Last fall I got to thinking about fate. I love the idea that the universe brings us to that perfect person, no matter how much we may fight it or how confused we may be. The concept stuck with me, and a week later I had the idea for *Her Christmas Surprise*. Both Keely and Lex are sure they know exactly what kind of person the other one is—and what they think of them. Watching their preconceptions fall away as they discover one another was fun. What a surprise when Keely finds out that the man she thought was the bad brother is the good guy after all!

I'd love to hear what you think of my tale. Drop me a line at Kristin@kristinhardy.com. And don't forget to keep an eye on the shelves as I'm hard at work on a trilogy set in Maine about a very special family of innkeepers in a very special town. Look for it in 2008. In the meantime, stop by www.kristinhardy.com for news, recipes and contests, or to sign up for my newsletter to be informed of new releases.

Enjoy!

Kristin Hardy

HER
CHRISTMAS
SURPRISE

KRISTIN HARDY

SPECIAL EDITION®

Published by Silhouette Books

America's Publisher of Contemporary Romance

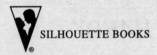

SILHOUETTE BOOKS

ISBN-13: 978-0-373-24871-1
ISBN-10:   0-373-24871-7

HER CHRISTMAS SURPRISE

Books by Kristin Hardy

Silhouette Special Edition

††*Where There's Smoke* #1720
††*Under the Mistletoe* #1725
††*Vermont Valentine* #1739
††*Under His Spell* #1786
**Always a Bridesmaid* #1832
Her Christmas Surprise #1871

Harlequin Blaze

My Sexiest Mistake #44
*Scoring #78
*As Bad As Can Be #86
**Slippery When Wet* #94
†*Turn Me On* #148
†*Cutting Loose* #156
†*Nothing but the Best* #164
§*Certified Male* #187
§*U.S. Male* #199
Caught #242
Bad Influence #295
Hot Moves #307
Bad Behavior #319

*Under the Covers
†Sex & the Supper Club
§Sealed with a Kiss
**Logan's Legacy Revisited
††Holiday Hearts

KRISTIN HARDY

had always wanted to write, starting her first novel while still in grade school. Although she became a laser engineer by training, she never gave up her dream of being an author. In 2002 her first completed manuscript, *My Sexiest Mistake*, debuted in Harlequin's Blaze line; it was subsequently made into a movie by the Oxygen network. Kristin lives in New Hampshire with her husband and collaborator. Check out her Web site at www.kristinhardy.com.

Acknowledgments

Thanks go to Ellen Zimiles, Co-Founder
and CEO of Daylight Forensic & Advisory,
David Johnson of the National White Collar
Crime Center, and Carmella C. Budkins, town clerk
of Greenwich, Connecticut

Dedication

To Gail and Charles,
for their infinite patience,
And to Stephen
All I ever wanted, all I ever needed…

Chapter One

"I think we should call off the wedding, Bradley. It just doesn't feel right to me. I'm sorry, but I think it's for the best." Keely Stafford gave a brisk nod. Calm, matter-of-fact, decisive. That was the right tone.

Too bad she was saying it to herself in an otherwise empty elevator rather than to her soon-to-be-ex fiancé's face.

Tonight, though, tonight at dinner she'd say it. She'd chosen a quiet, intimate restaurant where they could talk and where he was unlikely to protest too much. Do it in public, that was the thing.

In the meantime, stopping by to take her clothes and things from his midtown Manhattan apartment while he was at work would eliminate the need for any post-breakup visits. Not to mention keep her from chickening out, since the minute he noticed her stuff gone he'd have questions.

And Bradley always noticed everything.

She gave her head an impatient shake and pushed a strand of blond hair out of her eyes. She was twenty-five, for God's sake. She had a life, her own apartment, a career. If she had second thoughts about their impending marriage, then she needed to pay attention to them. She was old enough to know what she wanted.

At least she hoped so.

Keely walked down the hall to the door of Bradley's plush condo and reached into her purse for her keys. So she'd had a crush on him at twelve, back when they'd both lived in tiny, affluent Chilton and he'd been the golden boy of the country club. Back before he'd taken over his spot as top executive in Alexander Technologies, the company started by his great-grandfather.

And, yes, maybe she'd fallen for him hard when he'd walked back into her life when she was nineteen, but you couldn't build a marriage on infatuation. Things had felt wrong of late. Nothing she could put her finger on, just a niggling sense that if they went through with the wedding, they'd both be sorry.

The key slid into the lock with a quiet snick. And then she heard it.

A noise.

A noise, a loud thump inside what should be an unoccupied apartment. The hairs on the back of her neck prickled.

Leaning closer to the door, she focused. Seconds ticked by. And she heard it again. This time, it wasn't a thump, it was a human sound. Wordless, inarticulate. A groan.

Bradley.

Her heart began to thud. Had he fallen somehow, been hurt? Was he lying there alone, needing help and unable to summon it?

Swiftly, she opened the door and moved into the hall. Just as she opened her mouth to call out, the sound repeated, louder now that she was inside. And she stopped.

It wasn't a cry of distress. It wasn't the sound of someone in pain. It was the sound of a person in pleasure.

The sound of two people.

Shock paralyzed her.

"Oh, yeah, baby, like that, just like that," a woman's voice cried out with the now rhythmic thuds.

Keely stepped carefully on the marble floor of the entryway, trying to remain quiet. Not that it would matter, from the sound of things. They weren't listening for noises. They didn't care. They were completely caught up in one another.

She rounded the corner to the open door that led to the bedroom. And there, standing next to the bed with a woman's ankle against his neck, was Bradley, sweat gleaming on his naked shoulders.

Limber, the woman was definitely limber, was Keely's first distracted thought. She'd apparently perfected a position Keely hadn't even realized the human body was capable of. And Bradley was coming up with noises Keely hadn't ever heard from him—at least until he looked over and saw her standing in the doorway.

"Keely!" He pulled out of his partner and whirled around.

The woman cried out in protest.

Face hot, the blood thundering in her ears, Keely backed out of the room. The door. All she wanted to do was get to the front door and get out. Frantically, she snatched at the fingers of her left hand, struggling to pull off the engagement ring that now burned there. She didn't want anything of his touching her. She just wanted away.

"Keely, wait."

It was Bradley, wrapping his robe on.

"What, so you can finish?"

"It's not what you think. I can explain."

"You can explain?" She whirled to face him. "Explain what? Is this that special project you've been working on lately?"

"Keely, don't do this. I love you."

"I can tell," she said bitterly, glancing up at the woman who now stood in the doorway, wrapped in the emerald-green silk robe Bradley had brought Keely from Singapore. *Don't let it bother you. Don't let yourself care.*

"Look, I made a mistake."

"No, I'm pretty sure I'm the one who's made the mistake." It was like having battery acid running through her veins, burning, burning everywhere. The metal band of the ring slid off her finger, finally, and she slapped it down on the hall table. "I was feeling bad about doing this tonight but you've saved me the trouble."

"You're breaking up with me?" Bradley stared incredulously. "We're getting married in a month."

"No, Bradley, we're not getting married ever."

"Keely, don't be like this." He reached for her.

"Don't you touch me," she hissed. She wasn't sure what expression he saw on her face but he backed away.

"Keely, come on. Think about it for a minute. You'll be sorry if you walk out now."

"I'm already sorry, Bradley. Marrying you would only compound it."

Feeling light-headed, like she was in a dream—or a nightmare—she turned and walked out the door. She couldn't feel her feet touching the ground. There was a ringing in her ears, even as she descended in the elevator and walked out into the gray December day.

The midmorning street looked normal, cars passing, bits of snow still left from the recent storm, only a handful of pedestrians out. Most people were at work, where she should have been. Where she'd been sure Bradley would be. Keely strode down the sidewalk, not toward the subway that would take her to work but back toward her home and sanctuary.

Back where she could weep and let it all out.

So she'd been planning to break up with him. That did nothing to diminish the betrayal and hurt and humiliation of knowing he'd been cheating on her. Of seeing him with another woman, Keely's eyelids prickled and she sucked in a breath. She wouldn't cry, not here on the street. Home. She just had to get home and she'd be all right.

Sometimes what you thought you knew wasn't what you really knew at all. After all, she'd been certain when Bradley had walked into her mother's florist shop the summer before her senior year in college that she was falling in love. They'd stayed together nearly every weekend that summer, every time he drove up from Manhattan to Connecticut, every time she'd taken the train into town. It had been so perfect she'd been sure she was dreaming. Nothing could feel so good as being twined together with the golden, laughing Bradley.

She'd insisted on finding herself an apartment once she'd graduated and taken an accounting job with Briarson Financial in the city. She loved him, she was sure of it, but somehow, she hadn't wanted to live with him then, even though they'd spent all their time together. She'd wanted something of her own.

And then he'd proposed. "Why should we keep wasting money on cabs all over town?" he'd asked, sliding the ring on her finger. "I want you to be mine."

Keely had been so sure that they'd be deliriously happy the rest of their lives. And even though, nearly a year and a half later, she'd become increasingly certain that marrying him was the wrong thing to do, that did nothing to diminish the trauma of walking in to see him, *to see him* cheating with another woman.

Especially since they'd never had wall-banging, screaming wild sex like that. Their sex had always been quiet and, well, routine. Bradley had always seemed to enjoy himself and she'd enjoyed it, too. More or less. So it wasn't transcendent. Maybe she wasn't cut out for wall-banging sex. It hadn't seemed nearly as important as the other time they spent together.

But now, still seeing the scene every time she closed her eyes, she felt suddenly uncertain. Maybe what was missing between them wasn't something with Bradley. Maybe it was her. Did she not turn him on? Was she not woman enough?

Keely blinked hard and walked faster. Home. She just wanted to get home, call in to work and then have a good cry.

But when she mounted the steps of the tidy brownstone where she had a second-floor apartment, she found a crowd of uniformed police and other official-looking people milling about the lobby. That was the last thing she needed, news of a break-in or something in the building. Digging in her purse for her keys, she got into the elevator and stepped out a moment later onto her floor.

Only to see her front door wide-open.

It dizzied her. Her chest tightened so that she couldn't quite get a breath. She half ran the few steps down the hall. "What's going on?" she demanded. "What's happ— Oh, my *God!*"

Her apartment was completely ransacked, books, DVDs and CDs strewn about the living room, plants knocked over, the television taken off its stand and up-ended. From her vantage point, she could just glimpse the kitchen, cupboards yawning open and canisters spilling flour and sugar on the counter. "Did someone break in?" She moved to step inside.

The man at the door raised his arm to block her. "You can't come in here, ma'am."

"What do you mean I can't? I live here," she snapped.

"Ah." He eyed her speculatively. "If you'll just wait here…"

She wished she were the sort who wouldn't wait but would stomp into her apartment. That wasn't her, though, any more than throwing her engagement ring at Bradley would have been her, however much she'd ached to do it. Mind whirling, staring at the mess with sick horror, she waited.

A fortysomething man wearing a navy jacket and khakis appeared. "Are you Keely Stafford?" he asked.

"Yes, I am."

"Can I see some I.D.?"

With an increasing sense of unreality, she obeyed, getting out her wallet to show him the drivers' license she seldom had use for. "Is anybody going to tell me what this is all about?"

"Come in and have a seat," he said instead, inviting her into her own home.

Inside, the mess looked even worse. "My God, who did this? When did it happen? Everything was fine when I left here two hours ago." Numbly, she moved toward the hall that led to her bedroom, where the contents of the linen closet lay in a pile on the floor. Thieves? She didn't have much of value to steal, just her computer and her television, both of which were there. Vandals? But why?

"Miss, sit down. Please."

"Sit down?" Her voice rose. "This my home." She stalked over to the man on the couch, locking eyes with him. "If you or someone like you doesn't tell me what's going on in the next two seconds, I am going to pitch a fit the likes of which you've never seen before." And she realized as she said it, that it was true. "What's happened? Who broke in here?"

"We did."

And her legs gave out and she sat. "'We'? Who is we?"

"Federal agents. We're investigating a Bradley Alexander and we have reason to believe that he may have left items here germane to our case."

"Bradley?" she repeated incredulously.

The man flipped out a badge and a search warrant. "John Stockton, FBI. We have evidence that Bradley Alexander has not only been embezzling funds from Alexander Technologies, he's been laundering the money through a matrix of limited liability corporations—LLCs," he elaborated.

"I'm an accountant," she said shortly. "I know what an LLC is."

"I bet you do." He watched her, eyes appraising.

"What's that supposed to mean?"

"If you know anything about the operation, Ms. Stafford, it would be best if you cooperate with us. Mr. Alexander is facing criminal charges."

Down the hall in the bedroom, something fell with a crash. Keely flinched. "Cooperate? Am I under suspicion?"

"Let's just say you're a person of interest. You're his fiancée. You're an accountant and he's working a pretty complicated scheme. Even if all you did was give him advice, you need to tell us."

"Give him advice? I don't know a thing about any of this. And quite frankly, I find it hard to believe. Why would Bradley embezzle? He's rich. His family, the stock, his salary… He's chief operating officer of one of the biggest communications companies in the country. Why would he need to embezzle?"

"You tell me."

"I don't *know*," she burst out.

"Funny, his bookie does. So do his poker buddies."

"Poker? He plays in a home game, for fun."

"With a ten-grand ante. Between that and the bookie and the high-roller game in Atlantic City, he's lost millions over the past five years. Your fiancé's in one hell of a financial hole."

Her fiancé.

And immediately she was back in Bradley's condo, staring at his bare back as the muscles flexed, as he made love with another. Betrayal of the most exquisite kind. Without thinking, she sought out her now bare ring finger. "Ex," she said aloud.

"What?"

"Ex-fiancé."

The gaze Stockton turned on her was flat, skeptical. "You're due to be married next month. Tavern on the Green, according to my file."

"Not anymore. We broke up this morning, you can ask Bradley."

"We would if we could find him. Your…*ex*-fiancé has apparently skipped town."

She'd seen them before on the television news, victims of disaster, people overwhelmed by a mounting series of calamities, unable to cope, their expressions vacant with shock. Keely knew how they felt. First Bradley, then the search, then the reality of what he'd really done.

Done and dropped in her lap.

She couldn't say how long she'd been in the interview room, protesting over and over that she didn't know anything. And feeling the web draw tight around her. She supposed she ought to get a lawyer, but getting a lawyer would be admitting that it was really happening and she hadn't *done* anything.

But Bradley had.

He'd stolen tens of millions, they said. Alexander Technologies may have been family controlled, but it was still a public company. He hadn't been stealing from himself. He'd been stealing from shareholders. He'd ported funds from Alexander to fake vendors, LLCs he'd set up himself, to pay fraudulent charges for services that had never taken place, goods that didn't exist. That was just the start, though. Once the money was there, it had been funneled through a tangled web of corporations.

Corporations that listed her name on their boards of directors.

"I'm telling you I don't know anything about it," she'd protested.

"It's in your own best interest to work with us, Ms. Stafford," they'd said.

"I *am*." After hours of questioning, frustration had taken hold.

"How did he get your personal information?"

"He was my fiancé, for God's sake. He was in my apartment all the time. I didn't watch him every minute." And sometime when her back had been turned, when she'd been in the shower or kitchen, he'd found her social-security number and used it to link her to an embezzling and money-laundering scheme that might land them both in jail for a good long time.

Her saving grace was that they couldn't show she had any of the money. Mostly because she didn't. She'd known nothing about it, been no part of it, but the only person who could tell them that was Bradley, and sometime between the moment she'd stepped out of his door and the instant they'd simultaneously broken into her apartment and his, he'd disappeared. She'd been walking across town in that time. Bradley? Maybe some sixth sense had warned him. Maybe her walking in and finding him had gotten him out on the street sooner than he otherwise would have been.

She'd saved him from arrest. And in return, he'd slapped her in the face with betrayal. Then again, cheating on her was nothing compared with the scheme he'd embroiled her in. And now here she was, under investigation, her home invaded and ransacked, her life upended, her very freedom in jeopardy.

The door opened, startling her. It was Stockton.

"Ms. Stafford? We're finished with our questioning for now."

"I'm not under arrest?"

He shook his head. "You're free to go, but we'd like to be informed of your whereabouts. Don't leave town without telling us."

Of course. They'd want to watch her, see if she contacted Bradley.

She picked up her purse and rose.

"Ms. Stafford." Stockton held out a card. "If you find anything, if you think of anything that will help, call or e-mail. It's in both of your interests." His eyes watched her, unwavering.

"If I find out anything to help you, it'll be as much news to me as to you, Mr. Stockton," she said, and walked out without looking back.

* * *

Keely sat at her desk, staring at the parallelogram of sunlight that slanted in through the window and listened to the ringing of the phone held to her ear.

The way it hadn't rung for her in the two days since the police had searched her home.

"'Lo," said a laughing female voice.

"Lara," Keely said with a rush of gladness. "It's Keely."

There was a beat of silence. "Oh. Hi, Keely," Lara responded, the laughter gone now.

Lara Tremayne, her closest friend in the city. Lunches and gallery openings, committee meetings for fundraisers, they saw each other once or twice a week. Lara didn't, Keely noticed, ask what was new. She didn't have to. The newspapers and television news had taken care of that. Still...

Keely swallowed. "The cancer ball is coming up and we need to get the planning committee together."

"Oh, right. I meant to call you. The committee had a discussion—"

Keely's fingers tightened on the phone. "About what? I'm the chairperson."

"Yes, well, that's the thing. The feeling is that with your, er... With what's going on, well, we thought it was better if someone else took over."

"I see." Keely fought to keep her voice emotionless. "When did you make that decision?"

Lara hesitated. "The day before yesterday."

"When, exactly, were you planning to tell me?"

"Soon, Keely. I'm sorry. It's just awkward."

It hurt, Keely realized. She'd thought Lara was genuinely her friend. It looked like she'd thought wrong.

Lara cleared her throat. "Look, for what it's worth, I don't think you would ever have gotten into this without Bradley."

Keely bit back a reply as the phone line beeped and the caller ID panel flashed her boss's extension. "Look, Lara, I have to go."

"Me, too," Lara said in obvious relief. "Bye, Keely. I'll call you."

Yeah. Keely would hold her breath for that one. She pushed down the hurt and punched the button by the flashing light. "This is Keely."

"Keely, Ron. Can I see you in my office?"

Ron Arnold, her boss. Normally if he wanted to talk with her, he just stuck his head into her office when he walked by. This time, he was summoning her. With a sense of foreboding, Keely rose.

Since the day she'd walked in on Bradley, work had been the only part of her life that had been remotely normal. Normal, that was, if you discounted the crowd of paparazzi that camped out around the entrance of Briarson, snapping photos and shoving their microphones in her face. After all, it wasn't every day one of the hottest couples on the social scene got busted for white-collar crime. They couldn't find Bradley, so Keely was the next best thing, a photo to run next to the stories. "Fiancée and suspected accomplice Keely Stafford." Only she and Bradley knew their engagement was off.

"Sit down, Keely." Stocky and balding, Ron Arnold

had been her department head ever since she'd been at Briarson. "How are you?"

"Fine," she said automatically.

Arnold's gaze wasn't unsympathetic, though she wasn't sure pity was any easier to tolerate than the judgmental or frankly curious looks she got from the rest of the staff. "I'm sorry for what you're going through. It can't be easy."

Easy? Hounded by the press, watched by the authorities, returning at night to the shambles of her invaded home, no sanctuary anywhere? No, it hadn't been easy. "I'll survive," she said.

"Have you seen this?" He laid a folded copy of the *New York Post* down on his desk. It showed Keely walking into the building amid a crowd of reporters, her head down, her coat bundled about her. And on the wall behind her, clearly legible, was the Briarson Financial name.

"I'm sorry, Ron. I've tried getting here early, staying late. They're always after me, wherever I go."

"Hard to escape. Kind of like ticks that way," he said.

She gave him a grateful smile. "If it wasn't for this place right now, I don't know what I'd do. I think I'd go crazy."

"Keely." He hesitated. "There's been some concern from higher up in the organization. We've gotten calls from clients who've read your name in the papers. Some of the accounts you're working on."

Of course, she thought with a sinking heart. Keely Stafford, accountant at Briarson Financial, the center of an embezzling scheme. Not exactly the kind of thing a client wanted to hear.

"Your work here the past three years has been top notch. All of your reviews have been outstanding, even with the high-pressure accounts. We can't have our clients upset and doubting the organization, though. And every time you show up again in the press it only gets worse. I've been trying to keep things on an even keel but the higher-ups are demanding I do something. I think you understand."

Her lips felt cold. "Are you letting me go?"

"Not now," he said. "But we need you to take a leave of absence."

To where? The confines of an apartment that didn't feel like hers anymore? To the streets or a hotel, to be hounded by the press? "Ron," she began helplessly.

"Don't you have family in Connecticut?" Arnold cut in.

"Chilton."

"Good. Go there. Take the rest of the month. Go home. After all," he said, "it's Christmas."

Chapter Two

How had it happened? Lex Alexander wondered as he drove down the snow-bedecked main drag of Chilton, Connecticut. How was it he was back in Chilton, where everything looked just the same, from the herringbone parking on Main Street to the wrought iron arches that spanned the boulevard? The benches on the town common were green now, rather than the white they'd been twelve years before, but otherwise, little had changed in the time he'd been away.

Except him.

He'd hitchhiked, stowed away and knocked around the less savory parts of pretty much every continent on the globe since he'd turned his back on Alexander Technologies and everything that went with it. He'd sought out places most people in their right minds fled. And those who didn't faced them armed with a hell of a lot more than just their wits. He was nuts, some said.

If anything he did showed he was nuts, it was coming back to Chilton.

He'd known he was in trouble when he'd heard his mother's voice crackle over the phone. The fact that Olivia Alexander had tracked him down on the back side of nowhere was impressive in itself. In the places he frequented, he wasn't Aubrey Pierce Alexander III, he was just Lex, the man he'd made himself into since he'd turned his back on the role of heir apparent, turned his back on his autocratic bastard of a father. Or non-bastard, rather, since nobody had more impeccable breeding than the late Aubrey Pierce Alexander II—Pierce, to nearly everyone who knew him.

As for Lex, he'd been dubbed Trey at birth. Trey. Version 3.0. He hadn't even gotten a name of his own, let alone a life. Pierce had been relentless in his expectations and pressure. Any step outside the narrow box Pierce had defined earned discipline; the greater the rebellion, the greater the response. Aubrey Pierce Alexander III was by God going do what was expected of him.

What happened when an irresistible force met an immovable object? In Lex's case, what happened was that he walked away with little more than the clothes on his back. Walked away from the expectations, the family, the eight-figure trust fund. Walked away to remake himself.

Forget about Alexander Technologies. He'd been happy to leave that to his younger brother, Bradley, who'd always seemed to relish being the corporate G-boy and society-column staple.

But Bradley had apparently dug himself a hole that was threatening to swallow him up—and their mother, too. Maybe there were guys out there who could have ignored that desperate call and gone on with their lives, but Lex wasn't one of them.

No matter how tough he wanted to think he was.

God knew coming home was the last thing he wanted to do. If his father had been alive, it flat out wouldn't have happened, but the old man was gone and Lex knew damned good and well that his mother wasn't up to dealing with this on her own. Olivia Alexander might run the local DAR chapter and organize two-hundred-plate benefits with the efficiency of a general planning a military campaign, but she was unequal to facing the authorities and family ruin alone.

Lex pulled his rental car off onto a wide, quiet residential road bordered by stone walls, and felt the familiar sense of suffocation. Beyond the walls, at intervals, rose the stone and brick mansions of the Chilton *ton,* all decked out in their holiday finery.

The sudden urge hit him to just keep on driving. There were a dozen places he'd rather be, a dozen things he'd rather be doing. But first, he had to finish what he'd come here for.

And who knew how long that would take?

With a swing of the wheel that was as irritated as it was automatic, he pulled into the driveway that led to the Alexander estate and stopped at the intercom by the gates to press the button.

"Hello? Who is it?"

A maid's voice, unfamiliar, not surprisingly. What was he supposed to answer? Lex would draw a blank.

Aubrey Pierce III wouldn't do much better. "Trey Alexander," he said finally, and the gate buzzed open.

Trey Alexander. The person he'd thought he'd left behind. The life he'd thought he'd left behind.

He passed up the drive and pulled the car to a stop at the front steps of the house. Might as well get it over with, he thought, raking his dark hair back off his forehead as he headed up the steps. He'd done far tougher things than this in the years since he'd walked out. At least here, no one was likely to shoot at him, not even verbal missiles now that the old man was gone. If he hadn't known he was walking into a mess of trouble, he'd have even felt a bit of anticipation at seeing his mother again. Curiosity, at the very least. But there was trouble, he'd known it instantly by the tone of her voice. All she'd had to say was—

"Trey?"

She stood at the open door, staring at him. Twelve years had added some lines, but otherwise she looked the same, still trim, still stylish. Still richly, discreetly brunette—Olivia Alexander wasn't the type to give in to the gray. Except for his father, Olivia had always remained firmly in control of her world. Or maybe not, Lex realized as he kissed her smooth cheek and felt the slight tremble in the hand he held.

And then she was wrapping her arms around him, hard, in the warmest hug he could ever remember getting from her. "You came," she murmured. "I wasn't sure you would. It's been so long."

He hadn't been sure, either, just found himself on a plane without ever having made a conscious decision. He'd always scoffed at people's notions of family, at least when it came to his family. Maybe, just maybe, it wasn't so foolish after all.

When she stepped away from him, he saw the sheen of tears before she blinked them back.

"Hey," he murmured.

"I thought I'd never see you again," she said quietly. "Twelve years without a word."

"I'm here now."

"You're here now," she agreed.

He'd been the one to finally break the silence two years before. Stuck at a godforsaken Somali airfield, flipping through an out-of-date English news magazine, he'd turned the page to see an obit on his father. "The financial world mourns," the headline had trumpeted.

Lex hadn't, not a bit. But he'd spent a long night brooding over a bottle of whiskey and when the day had dawned he'd placed a call to his mother. Granted, three-month-overdue condolences weren't exactly timely, but better late than never. After that, he'd found himself with a strange compulsion to check in a couple of times a year. The conversations were awkward at times, full of silences during which they both groped for conversation, but he always found himself picking up the phone again.

And when the time had come, she'd figured out how to find him.

"Put your bag down and come sit," she said. "I'll have Corinne bring us something to drink."

It looked different, was his first thought as they walked through the house. Lighter, brighter. There was less of the oppressive heaviness the rooms held in his memories. Perhaps it had been his imagination. Or the shadow of Pierce. "The place looks good," he said as they walked into the living room, now inviting and airy.

She hesitated. "I changed a few things after your father passed away."

Interesting. Pierce had always insisted that his family home be kept as it had historically been—dark, ponderous furniture, ornate wallpaper, heavy drapes. Left to her own devices, Olivia had recovered the dark walls with pastels, pitched the dark green velvet window hangings of his youth for something softer. Luxurious, sure, and still traditional, but there was an inviting feel to the room, an openness it hadn't had before.

"I like it," Lex said as they walked to the chairs that overlooked the grounds. "You've done a nice job."

"It was time for something new."

Boy, wasn't that the truth? Too bad the something new involved legal action.

The maid brought coffee and for a few minutes the conversation was taken up by the safe and easy questions of cream and sugar; no, for him, in both cases. Then the maid bustled away and they settled back, watching one another in the silence.

"So." Olivia took a sip of coffee. "How was your flight?"

He gave a wry smile. "Which one? There were four."

"Any. All of them, I guess."

"Uneventful. Which is a fine thing in a flight." Especially the kinds of flights he habitually took. It had taken him days to work his way from the bush to Chilton, just one of the prices he paid for the life he led.

So different than here. He stared at the grounds outside the window, now covered with a light dusting of snow. "When did you get this?" He nodded at the drifts.

"A couple of days ago. A nor'easter. I lost two rose bushes. The gardener didn't get them properly mulched in time."

"Don't you hate when that happens?"

She blinked. "What?"

"Maybe they'll come back in the spring," he said instead.

"Perhaps. In the meantime, we've got all this snow. I don't know how much of it will stick, though."

"Why, is it supposed to warm up?"

"For a few days."

They both stared out at the snow as though it were the first time they'd seen it. The truth was, they didn't know how to be with each other after all these years. It was worse than being with a stranger—with a stranger, what he said wouldn't matter. Here, every word had resonance. The seconds ticked by. The silence stretched to the breaking point. Lex cleared his throat. "This is—"

"Is your—"

They stopped. "You first," Olivia said.

He nodded at his cup. "Good coffee."

"I'm glad you like it."

"One of the things they do well where I go is coffee."

She shook her head. "I don't know why you insist on going all these dangerous places."

"You can get in worse trouble in some neighborhoods in New York."

"I don't know why a person would go there, either."

He resisted the urge to say the obvious. Instead, he cleared his throat. "So how is the DAR?"

"Fine. We're working on the Christmas gala. It's only two weeks away."

"A lot to do."

"Oh, there is. Flowers, seating charts, music."

"Sounds like a lot of meetings."

"Always. I've had more cups of coffee in the past two weeks than you'd believe."

"Coffee can be good."

"It can. You always liked it, even when you were young. It's so strange to have you here," she blurted.

Out in the open, he thought. "It's strange to be here."

"You're a man." She shook her head. "When you left, you'd barely started shaving."

"Once a week, whether I needed to or not," he said ruefully, brushing his knuckles over his shadowed jaw.

"I guess time has a way of changing things."

"Generally," he agreed.

"I'm talking around it, aren't I?"

"You're allowed."

"Not when you've come all the way from Africa to help me. I'm sorry. I just didn't know who else to call."

"So where do things stand?"

"I assume you're referring to Bradley's legal troubles."

"Actually, I'm referring to yours."

It took her a moment to reply. "We have an appointment tomorrow at two with Frank Burton, to discuss the details."

Frank Burton, his parents' lawyer for as long as he could remember. "He on the case?"

"He's been in touch with the authorities and can tell us what they're doing to find Bradley."

"I assume you've tried the obvious stuff like calling his cell phone."

"The service is shut off."

"E-mail?"

"No reply." She shifted in her seat. "I'm sure there's a reasonable explanation."

"If there'd been a reasonable explanation, he wouldn't have bolted." And if she'd truly believed in it, there would have been no distress call. "Even if he's innocent, running makes him look guilty."

"I just can't believe that Bradley would do a thing like this on his own. It had to be that girl pushing him into it."

That girl. A wealth of disparagement in the words. "His fiancée? I thought you liked her. I thought she fit right in with this scene." Which made her about as far from anyone he'd want anything to do with as possible, but, hey, it wasn't his life.

Except for the fact that he was now thrown into the middle of it.

"I don't think she was good for Bradley."

He heard the obstinate denial in her words, knew that she wanted above all to avoid believing the worst of her son. "Mom," he began, "I don't think—"

She waved her hand, dismissing it. "There's no point in speculation. Let's wait for the details. They'll find him and we'll know everything soon enough."

Or not. Lex, of all people, knew how easy it was to go underground when you wanted to.

Olivia stood. Conversation over. "Why don't I show you to your room?"

They climbed the staircase, walked down the familiar hallways. And stopped at the door of his old room. "I hope it's all right. It's the only one that's made up, except for Bradley's. We turned yours into a guest suite after you left." She gestured at the pale green walls, the color of spring.

New beginnings.

Old memories.

Lex walked slowly inside, ignoring the new furnishings, heading toward the window. It had been the view he'd liked best, even when he'd been shut in for punishment. He could look across the grounds and off in the distance see a slice of blue where the sea glittered under the sun.

And dream about escape.

He heard Olivia walk up next to him.

"I missed you when you were gone," she said quietly, staring out at the sea on the horizon. "It's a terrible thing on a parent when their child disappears."

Guilt knifed through him. "Mom," he began helplessly, not knowing at all what to say. Knowing only that leaving had been his sole choice.

"I used to wonder every night where you were. If you were alive, if you were safe…whether you were somewhere wanting to come home. I always hoped that if you needed help, you'd tell me." Silence fell. And suddenly she was leaning her head against the cool window glass. "Why did he do it, Trey, why? Did we do something to him—to both of you?"

Oh, hell, he thought, and reached out a hand awkwardly to lay it on her back. "You didn't do anything to either of us."

"I let your father run roughshod over you."

"That's like saying you let the nor'easter hit. He did what he did. I did what I had to. Bradley made his decisions, too. None of it was anything you could have changed or stopped."

She straightened and turned to him with eyes that were dry, he saw in relief. "I don't know if that's true. I think you're being kind but I'm glad you're here."

"Not a problem." And suddenly he found himself reaching out to give her a hug that felt right.

"I just… I didn't know what to do," she said against his shoulder.

"Don't worry. We'll find Bradley, we'll figure it out. Everything's going to be okay."

He hoped like hell he was telling the truth.

"I can't say I'm sorry to see the back of that Bradley Alexander," Jeannie Stafford said to her daughter as she slipped a stem of baby's breath into an arrangement of gerbera daisies.

"I could have done with a different exit." With absent efficiency, Keely twisted ribbon together into a bow, added on an "Jeannie's Floral Creations" tag and handed it to her mother to tie onto the vase.

"I never liked him."

"He's not good enough for you, girlfriend. None of those Alexanders are, for that matter," said Lydia Montgomery, Jeannie's longtime clerk—and Keely's good friend since they'd begun working together in the shop's first days.

"He was always a little too pleased with himself. And now, look at what he's done to you," Jeannie fumed. "Look at the trouble he's gotten you into."

"And Olivia Alexander spreading rumors it was all your fault," Lydia added. She set aside the arrangement and began another.

"You don't know that she said that," Keely countered. She hoped not, she really hoped not. Olivia Alexander had seemed like one of the few genuine people in the social whirl. Keely had always thought Olivia liked her, that she'd approved of the match.

Lydia put her hands on her ample hips. "Well, Sandra Maxwell told me she overheard Little Missy Olivia talking when she was waiting on their table at Petrino's, and she usually tells me straight."

"I'm sure Olivia doesn't want to think that her son could do anything like that," Jeannie said. "What mother would? You'd hope that you'd raised them better."

"Well, she should wake up and smell the coffee." Lydia shook her head so hard that her red plait of hair swung back and forth. "She's been fooled. Everybody's been fooled."

Including yours truly, Keely thought. "Look, how about if I go get us some coffee and donuts?" she interrupted. If she didn't get out, she was going to go nuts.

Lydia and Jeannie gave each other a rueful look. "We're ranting, aren't we?" Jeannie asked.

"Well…"

"Oh, honey, I'm sorry." She gave Keely a hug. "He just makes me so mad, that's all."

"You deserve better," Lydia said.

"Why don't you take a break and go get us some coffee," Jeannie suggested. "We've got half an hour to finish the rest of these centerpieces for Lillian Hamilton's tea and you'll just distract us."

"I'll help when I get back."

"You're supposed to be relaxing."

"I relax better when I'm busy." Keely winked and walked out onto the street she could have navigated with her eyes closed.

Christmas garland festooned the trees, every shop was decorated, emphasis on quaint. Growing up, she'd always vainly hoped that her parents would move to the city, any city, just somewhere more exciting than Chilton. After all, they'd had the money to do whatever they wanted.

At least back then.

But Staffords had lived in Connecticut for decades, centuries, all the way back to the days of British rule. They weren't budging now.

Of course, things had changed in that time. Maybe they still lived in the big fieldstone house her great-great grandfather Clement Stafford had built in 1891, but the family money was gone, eaten away by the crash of 1987 and the subsequent bursting of the Internet bubble. Her father had many fine qualities, but stock-market savvy was not one of them. He'd ridden some big losers right down into the ground.

Oddly, he seemed happier now that the bulk of their holdings had been lost. Instead of facing a self-imposed pressure to increase the family fortune by the thirty or forty percent his predecessors had managed, he went to work every day to the shipping company that had brought him on as CEO. The company's stock kept rising and her father thrived.

As did the florist shop that Jeannie had launched right after the crash with the last of her own trust fund, hoping to keep the creditors at bay. She'd taken the skills that had won her Garden Club awards and parlayed them into a successful business. And if some of her DAR cronies looked down on her for working, she was happier being productive. So they'd had to sell off the houses in Provence, Vail and St. Bart's, the pied-à-terres in Paris and Milan. They were happy and they were comfortable, and that was all that mattered.

I never liked him. How had Keely missed that? She hadn't wanted to hear it, she acknowledged. Bradley had been her perfect golden boy, her teenage crush grown up, and she hadn't wanted to lose that illusion.

Instead, she'd lost all of them.

And now, her parents would wind up being out money on deposits for the reception and the flowers and the music, money they could ill afford to lose.

Then again, if things did~~n't go Keely's way, they~~ might find themselves spending a whole lot more helping her pay for a lawyer.

Keely shook her head. She wouldn't think about that now. She wouldn't think about the fact that she'd had to notify Stockton before she'd left Manhattan. A weekend. She'd work in her mother's shop, maybe go out for lunch with Lydia and give herself a weekend of thinking about nothing more demanding than irises and poinsettias. Come Monday, she'd tackle the whole mess and figure out how the heck she was going to reclaim her life. For now, she'd let the future take care of itself.

A few feet ahead of her, someone walked out the door of Darlene's Bake Shop, and the scents of fresh bread and coffee that wafted out after them had her mouth watering.

Some things never changed, Keely thought with a smile as she walked into the store. The same mismatched wooden and upholstered chairs sat around the same ragtag collection of tables in the café area. The walls were faded to the color of butter, still hung with the same antique pressed-tin signs and sepia photographs. The same wooden children's toys, knickknacks and memorabilia still sat on the blue shelves. And Darlene still stood behind the counter, a little older, maybe, a little wider, but with the same broad smile.

"Keely Stafford. I heard you were back," she said.

"You heard right. I figured I'd come spend the holidays with my parents."

"I bet they'll like that," Darlene said. "I'm sorry to hear about your troubles."

It was a simple comment, casually uttered. How was it that it had her eyelids prickling? "Thank you," Keely said, blinking. "It's going to be fine."

"I'm sure it will be. They'll figure out soon enough you weren't involved," Darlene said comfortably. "You just be patient. Now, what can I get you?"

"Got anything fresh out of the oven?"

Back in the kitchen, a timer peeped. "You must be a mind reader," Darlene said. "Give me just a minute."

As she bustled into the kitchen, the front door jingled. Automatically, Keely glanced over to see who had come in.

It was a man, dark and unshaven, rumpled-looking

in jeans and a black leather jacket. His build was rangy, his stride careless as he headed to the counter. His dark hair ran thick and undisciplined down to his collar, as though he didn't much care about what it did. When he got closer, she saw the lighter streaks of brown on the top. Sun, maybe? It would go with the tanned skin. Who had a tan in New England in December?

It was his eyes, though, that caught her attention, an almost unnatural green, smudged now with fatigue. There was something disturbing in those eyes, that direct gaze, something that gave her a little shiver deep down.

"'Morning," he said, coming to a stop beside her. "Can a guy get a decent cup of coffee here?"

Keely nodded. "You've come to the right place." He definitely didn't look like he belonged in Chilton. Just passing through, she was guessing. Or casing the joint. There was something about him, something unpolished and just a bit raffish that started a little buzz inside her. He reminded her of someone, an actor, maybe, with those cheekbones. That was probably why she kept finding herself sneaking looks at him.

He stared into the glass baked-goods case at the neat pyramids of croissants, scones, cherry Danish and doughnuts. "So what looks good here?"

You.

The thought came unbidden, just as he glanced up and caught her gaze on him. For a breathless instant, they looked at each other and she felt a sudden, surprising stir of heat. Her cheeks warmed. She would have known she was blushing even if she hadn't seen the slow smile spread over his face. Fortunately, Darlene came bustling back out of the kitchen to rescue her.

"Here we go, a fresh pan of corn muffins," she said. "I've also got carrot and blueberry and—" Her mouth fell open as she stared at the newcomer. "Trey? Trey Alexander? As I live and breathe. Just look at you!"

And recognition hit Keely with the force of a blow. Of course. Trey Alexander, Bradley's older brother, the one who'd been disowned. The one Bradley always joked had been voted most likely to in high school—most likely to be arrested, that was. With his faint flavor of lawlessness, Trey had always made her uneasy when she was younger. Granted, she hadn't seen him since she was fourteen, but still, she should have recognized him.

Darlene bustled out from behind the counter to hug Trey. "Look at you. You haven't been eating enough," she fussed. "Look how thin he is," she said to Keely.

Not thin, exactly. You could see the muscle and strength at a glance. It was more that he was stripped down, as though something had worn away the inessential parts, paring him down to nothing but muscle and bone. The cleft in his chin ran deep, his face all lines and planes and angles, with the sharpness of cheekbones pressing against the skin. It was the face of a hard man who lived in a hard world. A smuggler, Bradley had said, and he looked it. Only his mouth held any softness. Maybe that was why it kept drawing her gaze. It was a mouth that could fascinate, a mouth that could make a woman forget her better judgment.

At least until one corner of that mouth tugged up into the sardonic smile she remembered so well.

She knew that smirk, oh, she knew that smirk. It was the same one he'd given her when she'd seen him at the country-club tennis courts or around town, that hint of disdain, the curve of his mouth as though he were enjoying some private joke at everyone else's expense. Who was he to look down on her, anyway? What had he done that was so great, besides being disowned?

And now, here he was, popping up at the worst possible moment. She was already neck-deep in trouble, coping with the mess Bradley had made of her life. The last, absolutely last thing she needed was to deal with another Alexander. The last thing she needed was to deal with that smirk. Next, she'd walk out the door to run into Bradley's mother, Olivia, and her misery would be complete.

"A coffee, two lattes and three crullers," she said to Darlene. "To go."

"What's your hurry?" Lex asked, studying her.

Blond, slender, almost luminous, there was about her a bit of that smooth elegance the women in Chilton always had, the result of salon pampering, expensive cosmetics, luxurious clothing. Amazing what money could buy.

"I've got to get back."

"To where?"

"Her mother's florist shop," Darlene broke in. "Although I guess that all happened after you left. You're behind the times, Trey. Or I guess it's Lex you go by now, isn't it?"

"Lex?" the blonde repeated. "That's new."

"Short for Alexander," Darlene explained. "Our Trey grew up."

And he saw. Older than he remembered, thinner and somehow more brittle, yet more beautiful even so.

Keely Stafford, his brother's fiancée.

"Well, I'll be damned," he said.

Lex had never deluded himself that he could come into town and avoid everyone but Darlene and his mother. He'd never expected to run into Keely Stafford, though. Olivia had babbled about her leading Bradley astray. Lex wasn't so sure of that. Bradley was quite capable of getting into trouble on his own; he didn't need Keely to help him.

Which didn't mean Lex hadn't always found her irritating on general principles. She was part of the perfect plastic world he'd walked away from, one of the twin-set-wearing, country-club tennis players headed off to get their Mrs. degrees at college. He didn't want to remember seeing her at the club when he was almost eighteen, just before he'd left home for good. She'd been maybe fourteen if she was lucky, on the court in a little white skirt, a disturbingly innocent sexuality in her coltish legs and unself-conscious strides.

She might have been a kid then, but she was all grown up now. And if she'd disturbed him then, he had a pretty good feeling that now she could send him right around the bend. There was something about her, not quite beautiful but interesting. She'd photograph well, he thought. At first glance, she seemed cool, controlled—smooth blond hair, brows perfectly arched above soft gray eyes, slightly tilted cheekbones that threw just enough shadow to be intriguing.

But there was something else about her, something hovering in her gaze, something about the way her mouth managed to be both delicate and enticing at the same time. It was a combination that caught at a man's imagination, a combination that might make a man do anything to try to unlock the secret.

Even steal millions, if he had to.

Maybe Olivia wasn't so far off base after all.

"I thought you were supposed to be in New York," he said, without realizing he was going to.

"And I thought you were supposed to be smuggling in Outer Mongolia," she replied coolly.

It amused him. Almost. "I came home to help my mother with this whole legal mess. I guess you'd know something about that."

Her chin came up at his words. "What's that supposed to mean?"

"Nothing more than it sounds like. I'd hope you know about it. Bradley is your fiancé, after all."

"Ex-fiancé," she said, with a bit more of an edge.

Interesting. "Ex? When did that happen? Before the feds showed up or after?"

She flushed and turned to take the bag and the coffee carrier Darlene handed her. "I'm not sure it's any of your business."

"This entire mess is my business whether I want it to be or not. You and Bradley are the whole reason I'm here."

Her stare was bland as she walked over to the ledge that held sugar and creamer and spices. "For what, our wedding? How touching." She sifted a bit of cinnamon over her latte before taking a drink of it.

"Don't be cute. There's trouble and you know it. My mother called me to help out."

"Who, Bradley?"

"Both of them."

"The only way to get Bradley out of trouble is to find him." She put the cover back on the cup.

"So why don't you?"

"Find him?"

"You've got to have an idea where he is."

"I haven't a clue. Anyway, you'd probably do better at finding him than I would. You're another one who knows how to leave and stay gone, from what I hear."

"And now I'm back."

"So you are." She set the muffin bag in the middle of the carrier and turned toward the door. "And now I'm gone."

He followed her outside. "Back to New York? Doesn't seem like it would be too much fun right now." He'd caught sight of the lurid headlines in the airport. Contempt had had him ignoring the scandal sheets with their blurred paparazzi pictures or he probably would have seen Keely. That was where the brittleness came in, he was guessing.

"It's none of your business where I go. The engagement's off. I'm done with Bradley. And the rest of you. If it weren't for your brother, I wouldn't even be back in this town."

Just as Bradley was the reason he was back. Irritation pricked at him. "Tell me where Bradley is and we can all go home."

"I told you, I don't know."

"You can't really expect me to believe that."

"I don't care what you believe."

She moved to turn away but he captured her free wrist in his hand. Her skin was smooth under his fingers, and impossibly soft. "Not so fast. We need to talk."

She turned on him. "We don't have anything to talk about."

"Oh, I think we've got plenty."

For a breathless instant, they stood, toe to toe, gazes clashing. The seconds ticked by, then abruptly, surprisingly, her eyes darkened. Desire punched through him, sudden and unexpected.

Deliberately, she glanced down to where he held her. "Let me go." Her voice was icy calm.

He wondered if she had any idea how hard her pulse was thudding against his fingers.

Well, well, well, he thought, Keely Stafford wasn't nearly as cool as she tried to pretend. It hadn't been his imagination. There was heat under that calm, composed exterior.

"All right." He was surprised at the effort it took to make his fingers release her. "For now," he said.

"For good," she countered. "I've had enough of you Alexanders to last me a lifetime."

"You haven't had me."

"You're the last one I need." Her voice was low.

"Maybe," he said, leaning closer and brushing one fingertip over her chin just to feel her skin. "But don't think you've seen the last of me."

"Go to hell," she snapped, and walked away.

And he stood and watched her go.

Chapter Three

It was infuriating, Keely thought the next morning as she did a flip turn at the end of the lane in her parents' indoor pool. He'd put his hand on her and she'd just stared at him like some idiot. Not like some idiot, like some ditzy thirteen-year-old staring at the football captain. So maybe Trey Alexander—excuse her, Lex—exuded a rough kind of charm, but she wasn't about to let it work on her. One Alexander brother had been enough.

One Alexander brother had been too much. Men, in general, were too much for her just then. She stroked rhythmically, trying to let the soothing slide of water wash away the tension. There was nothing to put a person off relationships quite like walking in on their fiancé in flagrante delicto. Every time she closed her eyes she could see it. How long had it been going on? How long had he been running around behind her back, making love with another woman? Or other women, plural. How many of them had there been?

And had he ever come to her bed from another's?

In a swift, fluid movement, she pushed up out of the pool. It would be a long time before she trusted her judgment again when it came to men. It would be a long time before she gave herself a chance to.

Keely rose to walk toward her towel and found it held by a tall, sandy-haired man with a bemused smile. "Need this, pumpkin?"

She grinned at her father. "I'd give you a hug but I'd get you all wet."

"It doesn't matter," Carter Stafford said, wrapping the thick, white towel around her and giving her a quick squeeze. "I'm working from my home office today."

"Is that why the khakis?" she asked, squeezing him back. Above them, light danced on the ceiling where it was reflected by the surface of the water.

"Nope, I wear those pretty much every day. The perks of being the boss." He winked.

"You still like it, don't you?" She stepped away to towel off her hair.

"Beats working for a living."

"Speaking of work, I should get over to the shop and help Mom."

"You could just relax, you know. You've been here less than a week."

"And this is one of the busiest seasons of the year." She hung the towel around her neck. "Especially with her being out tonight."

"Can I help it if this is when my company scheduled the Christmas party?"

Her lips twitched. "You are CEO."

"You think they ask me about these kinds of things?" He snorted. "Besides, I know your mother and her business. There's never a good time, especially at the holidays."

"It's a good thing that I'm here to fill in, then, isn't it?" Keely said over her shoulder as she walked through the French doors that led into the main house.

He followed her. "Why don't you come with us, instead? Give me a chance to show you off."

She shook her head. "The town tree lighting is tonight. People will be in a buying mood, so we'll want the shop open." Not just for flowers, but for the gift area where they sold ornaments and cards, jewelry and the kinds of foolish, pretty things that made Christmas morning surprises.

"All for the sake of the shop, eh?" Carter asked. "Nothing to do with the fact that you've never missed a tree lighting yet?"

"Nothing at all."

"I see. Maybe we should stay here and go with you. After all, I am CEO, as someone just pointed out to me."

"And as such you have responsibilities." She grinned. "You're just going to have to tough it out and go swill champagne and caviar with the other swells. I'll hold down the fort."

"You're supposed to be taking a rest cure," he scolded.

"If I just sat around, I'd go nuts. I'm kind of like my parents that way. Got to be useful."

"You had to start working too soon," he said, his smile fading a bit.

"Dad, everyone works in high school and college."

"You, of all people, shouldn't have had to."

She flashed a smile and rose on her tiptoes to kiss his cheek. "It was good for my character." She waggled her eyebrows and did her best Groucho Marx imitation. "And I am nothing, if not a character."

"She could lose the *house?*" Lex stared across the smooth, polished ebony of the desk and into the eyes of Frank Burton, his parents' longtime personal attorney.

"That can't be possible." Olivia spoke up from where she sat by Lex in a powder blue suit and pearls.

"You're listed on the boards of five of the LLCs Bradley set up. The shell corporations, I mean, the ones he used to funnel the money away." He glanced at the sheet before him. "Correction, five that they know of. They're quite certain there are more."

"But I don't remember any of this," Olivia said positively. "And I would have. I don't just sign things without reading them, you know."

"He wouldn't have needed to have you sign, not if he had access to your social-security number and your passport. Did he?"

That stopped her. "I don't know. He had access to my office. I suppose he could have found anything if he was looking for it."

"At any rate, that's only part of the trouble. The most damning fact is that he funneled money through your bank account. He deposited five million dollars on ten occasions over the past two years." Burton held up a thick manila folder. "It's all documented."

Olivia stared. "Five million dollars?"

"Times ten. Fifty million, all told. The question is, why? Do you have something to show cause? A receipt, maybe? Records of business transactions? It's important that we demonstrate the transfers were legit."

"I didn't… I don't know anything about it," she said helplessly.

Burton frowned at her over his glasses. "They were five million dollar deposits. Granted, the sums you receive from your quarterly dividends and real-estate holdings are as big, if not bigger, but still, where did you think it came from? And didn't you wonder when it was transferred out?"

"A bank error?" she suggested.

Burton gave her a skeptical stare. "Ten times? Olivia, if you know something, now's the time to tell us."

"I don't… I can't…I—" She turned to Lex, a thread of desperation in her voice. "Your father always did our finances. You know how he was. When he passed away, I was just…" She firmed her lips. "There was so much to see to, the funeral arrangements, notifications, wills. Bradley offered to take care of things. It was a relief to hand it over to him. And then it just became habit," she trailed off.

"You played right into his hands," Burton said. "He used his access to launder money through your accounts, bringing it in from his shell corporations and porting it out to an accomplice."

Olivia closed her eyes for a moment. "I can't believe he'd do it."

"The feds can." Burton's expression was grim. "They've got enough evidence to consider you involved. That means all of your possessions and holdings are subject to seizure."

"All of it?" She paled. "Everything?"

Lex leaned forward. "But she didn't keep the money."

"Not at that step. They don't know where it eventually wound up, though. She could still have it somewhere."

"And on those grounds they can take her house?"

"They can take it all," Burton assured him. "Not right away, of course. First, they've got to get to the bottom of the whole scheme, and it's tangled enough that it could take a year or more. Quite frankly, that's the reason they're sure his fiancée is involved."

His fiancée? Keely? Lex frowned. "What do you mean?"

"She's an accountant, didn't you know? Worked for Briarson Financial. It's unlikely someone like Bradley would have known enough to carry off this kind of scheme on his own and get past his internal auditors. With someone of her background helping him cook the books, though, it would be a cakewalk."

"She's an accountant?" Lex had assumed she'd majored in something like English literature or art history, one of those degrees for the ladies who lunched. Clearly, he'd been mistaken. "So they think she had something to do with it?"

"They're almost certain of it. Mind you, they haven't got any evidence yet, but they will. Trust me, they will."

"If she's involved, she's in a position to clear my mother's name, right?" Lex asked. Forget about vulnerable mouths and shadowed eyes. If she had the answers, he'd worm them out of her.

"Any testimony you can get from someone who's involved would certainly help Olivia's case," Burton answered. "What we really need is to find your brother but he seems to have gone into the wind."

Keely, though, Keely was right here.

"We should talk to the fiancée," Burton said.

Lex felt a slow-burning anger awake. "Leave it to me." And this time he'd get some straight answers, before his mother lost everything she had.

Olivia took a breath and straightened her posture in a move Lex recognized. No tears, no weakness here. "What happens next, Frank?"

"Nothing immediately. They'll keep investigating until they've got it all worked out, put their case together. Then it'll go to trial. With or without Bradley."

"So we have time," Lex said.

"Some. The sooner you can get the fiancée to come clean, the better off your mother will be."

And the sooner he could go back to his life, escape the morass that was already beginning to suck him in.

Abruptly, he rose. "Then I guess I'd better get on it," he said, holding his hand out to Burton.

"You hear from Bradley, you let me know immediately," the lawyer said as he walked them out.

"You know it."

The carpet in the hallway outside Burton's downtown Stamford offices was thick and plush underfoot, the color of the brandy Pierce had favored. Ahead, light streamed through the glass walls that surrounded the ten-floor atrium lobby.

"I just can't believe it was Bradley," Olivia said as they waited for the elevator. "She must have pushed him into it."

She might have been involved, but Lex had a pretty good idea nobody pushed Bradley anywhere. There was one trait they'd both inherited from their father, his stubborn single-mindedness. It had fueled Lex's rise to the top of a difficult and dangerous field. It had also helped Bradley take a controlling position in Alexander Technologies, the position that had let him get away with his crimes.

For a while.

"Mom," Lex said gently, "no one made Bradley run."

But if Keely Stafford had helped him, then she knew how to untangle this rat's nest. And she damned well needed to start talking.

"Bradley doesn't know what to do with the mess she's gotten him into," Olivia maintained, but her voice was uncertain.

"Have you ever, in your entire life, seen Bradley do anything he didn't want to do?"

"He couldn't have done this on his own. I won't believe it."

Translation: she didn't want to.

She had to face it, though, or she'd never get past it. "No one made him gamble, Mom." Lex kept his voice gentle. "You saw the statements from the pit bosses. Brad got in trouble, he wanted out, and he wasn't too concerned about how."

Abruptly, the starch went out of Olivia's posture and for just a moment she sagged against the railing that looked down over the lobby. "What am I going to do?" she whispered. "They're going to take it all. How could he do this? How could he leave me with nothing?"

And now she did cry. All he could do was gather her against him and stand there, helplessly patting her back. No. Not helpless, never helpless. There was a way to fix this and he would find it.

Starting with Keely Stafford.

"Are you sure you're going to be all right here tonight?" Jeannie stood behind the counter at the flower shop, buttoning her coat.

"I'll be fine. I've got Lydia coming in later to help."

"The mistletoe for the novelty hangers is on the table."

"I know. I was the one who put it there, remember? Now git." Keely draped her mother's scarf around her neck. "You've got a party to primp for. How else are you going to get to dissect the centerpieces if you're not there?"

"What would make you think I'd do such a thing?" Jeannie asked.

Keely grinned. "I know you too well. Have a great time." She kissed her mother's cheek.

"Thank you again. And don't spend the whole night working. Go out and watch the tree lighting. You should have some fun."

"Out," Keely ordered, pointing at the door.

"I'm going," Jeannie said hastily.

Keely watched the door close behind her. In a while, Lydia would show up and their gab fest would begin. For now, Keely had the shop to herself. She breathed in air scented with roses, carnations, hyacinths, and remembered.

The shop had defined her life in so many ways. One minute, the Staffords had had money, country club memberships, prestige. The next, she'd found herself pitching in to help pay the bills, filling out reams of scholarship and loan applications to cover college. The long, hot, lazy summers she'd grown up with had been replaced by cool days in the shop, wearing the tailored black shirt and trousers that were the uniform at Jeannie's.

Then Bradley had come through the door to buy a bouquet for his mother. And Keely had fallen as deeply into infatuation with him as she had at fourteen, when he'd been the star of the country-club tennis court and she'd prayed for him to ask her to play doubles with him.

Now, five years later, she was back at the florist shop, tying a ribbon on an arrangement of mums. All those years of study, the internships, the work at Briarson, blown apart by Bradley. She struggled to push down the surge of anger as she carried the vase into the glass-fronted, walk-in refrigerator that held orchids, roses, daylilies and the other exotics.

Behind her, a jingling signaled the entry of a customer. With a sigh of resignation, Keely turned.

Only to see Lex Alexander.

Suddenly, abruptly, the shop felt very small. And very empty. He didn't hesitate, didn't look around at any of the arrangements. Just headed straight for her.

Keely met him at the door to the refrigerator. The

shallow space in front of the tiers of flowers was far too small for two. "Looking for some flowers?" she asked.

"Looking for you."

He was taller than she'd realized the day before, topping her five ten so that she found herself staring at his chin. In defense, she raised her own. "I'm working."

"The shop's empty. We need to talk."

His eyes were dark, turbulent as he stared down at her. She felt that same stir of awareness she had before. Her pulse thudded in her ears. He was too big, too strong. Too *there*. She took a breath and pushed past him. "I have things to do," she said without turning.

"Fine. I'll talk with you while you do them."

Keely made a noise of frustration and walked to the counter. "I don't see what we've got to talk about."

"How about this little scheme you've got going with Bradley, for a start."

She did look at him, then. "I don't have any scheme going with Bradley."

"The feds say you do."

"The feds don't have a shred of evidence." Because there was none.

"They've got your name on the boards of some LLCs."

"They've got your mother's name on those boards, too," she countered.

"Why do you think I'm here? I need to know what you know."

"I don't know anything. I already told you, I'm not a part of this. Bradley was on his own." She walked into the back and told herself she wasn't fleeing.

It didn't matter. He followed her. "Oh, come on.

You're his fiancée, you're an accountant. You know as well as I do he couldn't figure this out alone."

"Nice that you have such a high opinion of him." She didn't look at him, just picked up some scarlet-berried holly off the counter and jammed it into a small vase to get it out of the way. Lex still made her as uneasy as he had when she was a teen, only now it was overlaid with something else, a humming tension she didn't want to think too much about.

"My opinion doesn't matter," Lex said. "What matters is that my mother could lose everything because of what he's done. I need to get her out of this and to do that, I need you."

Keely snatched up one of the branches of mistletoe that lay on the worktable and began snipping off sprigs. "What you need is Bradley, and no, before you start in on it again, I don't know where he is." The snap of the clippers punctuated her words. "I don't know anything about any of it."

"I find that hard to believe."

"And I don't really give a damn." She slapped down the clippers. "I've got the feds on my tail, a boss who told me to get lost and an apartment that's been torn apart, thanks to your brother. I could give a hang what you believe." Jaw clamped, she snatched up the scissors and began chopping off hanks of red ribbon to bind the mistletoe. "Now, either buy something or get out of this store."

Lex studied her for a minute, arms folded. "All right, let's say you didn't have any part of it. If that's true, then it's in your interest as much as ours to get to the bottom of this thing."

"Sure, I'll get right on that. Let me just find my magic wand."

"Look, you're an accountant. Even if you didn't have anything to do with it, you should still be able to follow the trail. Maybe you'll find something the big boys missed. Clear your name and my mother's. As his fiancée, I'd think you'd want to get to the bottom of it."

"He's not my fiancé," she said tightly. "I told you, we broke up the morning of the raid."

"Perfect timing."

"No, perfect timing would have been two years ago when we first started dating," she snapped. "Forget it, okay? If I want to play detective, I can do it on my own."

"Not if you want access to my mother's papers."

"What for?"

He shrugged, toying with a piece of mistletoe. "He used her accounts as part of his scheme. You might just find the key to something."

"Your mother is never going to give me access to her papers. From what I hear, she blames me for the whole thing. First her, then you. What could possibly make me want to work with people who don't even believe me?"

"Change her mind," Lex suggested. "Change mine."

"Why should I? Why should I care what either of you think?" Keely reached over for a sprig of mistletoe.

And his hand landed on hers, stopping her dead. "It's in both of our interests."

Heat bloomed up her arm. For an instant, she didn't move, couldn't. His fingers were warm, his palm hard. And all she could do for a helpless instant was wonder what it would feel like on her naked body.

"Think about it," he suggested.

For a bewildered second, Keely wondered how he could possibly know what was in her mind. Then she realized what he meant, and swallowed. "Thanks, but no thanks. And like I said, it's time for you to go."

He removed his hand. "Let me know when you change your mind."

"If," she corrected.

"When."

"Try never," she retorted.

He laughed, his teeth very white against his dark skin. "I'll be around when you're looking for me."

Chapter Four

Lex stepped out onto the sidewalk into the late afternoon. The last bits of snow from the nor'easter crunched underfoot. The setting sun stained the sky ruddy.

And he could still feel the softness of Keely's skin against his palm.

She hadn't told him anything he needed, he reminded himself. What she'd told him was to take a hike. He should have been frustrated, but somehow all he kept focusing on was how she'd felt, fragile yet strong.

And the way that mouth of hers might taste.

He gave an impatient shake of his head. There were many dumb things he could do, but getting involved with his brother's fiancée—or ex-fiancée—pretty much landed at the top of the list. He didn't even like the woman. He'd never had any use for her or her Junior League kind.

So why did he find himself distracted by wondering whether if he kissed her, the Junior League girl would turn into a woman, hungry and urgent?

Ridiculous. He'd kissed plenty of women in his time. He didn't need to kiss one more, no matter how much she kept popping up in his thoughts. What he needed to do was get his mother off the hook and get gone, because the longer he stayed, the more bound he felt—by the need to help Olivia find someone to run her finances, by the questions about her estate. The maid had shown up in his room that morning with his father's old tux, to measure him for alterations so Lex could wear it to the Christmas gala as Olivia's escort.

Charity balls and investment advice weren't him. Servants and tuxedos weren't him. He was about tramping through bush and desert and jungle, looking to capture that elusive moment that could encapsulate a place and time, giving people an immediate, gut-level understanding of what was happening in their world.

And maybe after fourteen years, he was starting to get tired of the dirt, the exhaustion, the crappy beds and food, starting to get soul-deep tired of man's seemingly endless capacity for destruction. That just meant he needed a break, that was all. It sure as hell didn't mean he needed to come back to Chilton and take up where his father and Bradley had left off.

He stared at the fading light on the horizon and thought of sunsets along the equator, where the transition from dark to light took place in the blink of an eye. Where the sunsets and sunrises hit at the same time every day, no matter the season, because the seasons were just warm and warmer and you slept naked in the heat. And that quickly, images of Keely were back dancing in his head.

To derail his thoughts, he pushed open the door to Darlene's.

Darlene stood behind the baked-goods case with a white bag in her hand as she filled the order of a harried woman trying to buy muffins and manage the children hanging on to her legs.

"Two corn, four blueberry— Tommy, *stop,*" the woman snapped. "Two bran and two…" She paused for thought, studying the baked goods in the case.

Darlene shook the bag a bit. Impatient, Lex thought with a smile. "Apple banana?" she suggested. "Carrot?"

"I'd go with carrot," Lex said, stepping forward. "They're the best. I swear, I could smell them all the way over in Tanzania."

The woman stared at him. "Cranberry," she muttered.

Darlene raised an eyebrow at Lex. "About time you came back. You hardly even said hello yesterday," she complained, dropping the customer's final two muffins into the bag. "And what's this about Tanzania? The last postcard I got from you was from Chechnya."

"I thought I'd head somewhere warm for a while." Darfur, to be precise, at least until he'd seen all he could take. Taking photographs of endangered species being slaughtered was a hell of a lot harder to stomach when they were human beings.

With an almost physical effort, he turned his thoughts back to the present.

"Well, I still think you're too skinny, wherever you've been. Here, take one of these. No, two." Darlene shoved a pair of carrot muffins to him before she went back to her customer.

Grinning, Lex watched her hand the woman change. Back when he'd lived in Chilton, Darlene had been one of the rare adults he could tolerate, one of the few who hadn't treated him like either a brainless clone of a previous generation or a felon in training. So he'd broken a few rules; that made him a misguided kid, not a criminal, whatever anyone had said. Darlene hadn't cared. She'd just treated him like a person and he'd adored her for it.

"So what's Tanzania like?" she asked, pushing a cup of coffee toward him.

"Beautiful. So open and gorgeous it takes your breath away. You've got a postcard coming." With a pair of smooching baboons on the front, he recalled.

"It'll go with the rest of my collection."

Glancing over her shoulder, he saw the wall behind her was decorated not with comic signs but with a rainbow patchwork of postcards—his postcards—sent from all over the world. She'd kept them all, he realized.

And felt an unexpected stab of an emotion he almost didn't recognize.

When he'd walked away from home, he'd left behind all the strings and entanglements, and he'd kept it that way. It was easier. What little companionship he needed, he got from his colleagues, his editors, or passing involvements with women who wanted little more than an occasional warm body to hold in the darkness. It was a life that suited him.

And if in the odd lonely night on the back side of the world he felt something was missing, whose business was it but his?

Except that now he was staring up at all those damned postcards, tacked up there on the wall, as Darlene waited on another customer.

He'd never sent letters to his mother, not wanting to make her the target of Pierce's anger. He hadn't really thought about why he sent them to Darlene; he wasn't sure he wanted to now. It was easier to take his coffee to a table and leave Darlene to her customers.

He didn't need one more tie in Chilton.

Keely stood at the front of the flower shop, hanging the bundles of mistletoe on the shop's eight-foot pine Christmas tree. She'd gotten them all done pretty quickly after Lex had left. Better to keep busy than to think about that moment he'd touched her. It was nothing, of course. She'd been emotional anyway ever since things had blown up with Bradley. Of course she'd overreact to everything. She'd just been angry with him.

That was all.

Through the glass window at the front of the shop, she watched the early winter twilight fade into darkness. It was time for the evening commute, time for people to start flowing onto the Chilton common for the annual lighting of the town's Christmas tree. It was the first official shopping night of the season and they'd get plenty of business from it. That was what she needed to focus on, not her problems.

Not a pair of dark, unsettling eyes and a voice that sent something shivering through her.

The bell at the door jingled. She glanced up to see a face she recognized from that nightmare day Bradley had left: John Stockton, the federal agent investigating Bradley.

She blinked.

"Evening." He stepped across the flagstone floor of the shop, looking around approvingly at the vases of arranged flowers, the hanging plants, the gardening gear, the gift shop.

"Aren't you a little far from your turf?" she asked.

"Not so you'd notice," he said equably. "I live in Stamford. You're on my way home."

"I'm not inside your jurisdiction, though."

"My jurisdiction's wherever it needs to be. I'm not a cop. Nice place," he added, looking around. "I hear your mother started it a few years back."

"After my family lost our money. You forgot to add that part."

"No." He looked at her steadily.

"I see. So I have motive, is that it?"

"You tell me."

"I don't steal. Besides, I've got a job and a trust fund. I don't need to."

"If you say so."

"Maybe it's time for me to get a lawyer."

He shrugged. "If you like. I'm just here to say hello. You're not under arrest. Yet."

"Have you found Bradley?"

He stopped to look at a display of sun catchers. "No, again. Your fiancé's good at laying low."

"Ex," she corrected.

"That's right. Ex. You heard from him?" He turned his gaze on her.

Flat. Skeptical. The same way he'd looked at her in the interrogation room. "Not a peep. Did you talk with his family?"

"I'm putting my money on you."

"Then you probably already have my phones tapped and people watching me. If Bradley calls me, you'll know." She finished hanging the mistletoe and walked back behind the checkout counter. "You've got nothing to worry about."

"But maybe you do."

Her stomach tightened. "What's it going to take to convince you that I wasn't a part of this?"

"Vilis Skele," he said.

Keely blinked. "What?"

"Vilis Skele."

"I haven't a clue what you're talking about."

"Who. He's a Latvian arms dealer. Does a lot of business in the Middle East. Lives here part-time, mostly to simplify his business dealings."

"Oh, sure, I guess lots of Latvian arms dealers do that."

"Particularly when they're getting money laundered."

And now she saw it. "You mean, Bradley—"

"Laundered upward of two hundred million for him over the past year and a half," he finished for her. "That we know about, anyway. It could be more. He could be a cottage industry for all we know. Slick operation, by the way. He set up LLCs for Skele, some of them clients of Alexander Technologies, some of them vendors. Some of them clients and vendors for those LLCs. Skele sent in money from the client LLCs and got it back through payments to the vendor LLCs."

"Maybe they're real."

His gaze hardened. "You, of all people, should know that's not true. You're on the boards of several of them. Skele means *slice* in Latvian," he added conversationally. "He's slit the throats of twelve men that we know of."

Keely groped for the chair behind her. An arms dealer? "It doesn't make any sense."

"Sure it does. Your Bradley got in deep enough while his father was still alive to arrange for some, shall we say, high-interest financing?"

"A loan shark," she said numbly. "You're talking about a loan shark."

"Bingo. Papa died and Bradley starting siphoning off money from the corporation, but he couldn't do it fast enough. Then he met Skele at a high-roller game in Atlantic City. I've got the dealer who introduced them. They got very cozy, she tells me. The dates correspond with the incorporation dates of most of the LLCs."

"I'm not a part of this."

"Enough, all right?" Stockton's voice rose. "This isn't just embezzling and SEC violations you're looking at anymore. This is the big leagues and anyone involved is going to go away for a long time. *You* could go away for a long time. Unless you cooperate."

"I've told you…"

"And I don't want to hear it anymore," he broke in.

"Your boy crossed the line. He's going down and he might just take you with him if you don't watch it."

"This is harrassment. You don't have a shred of evidence apart from my name on some boards."

"I'm just asking a few harmless questions," he said. He started away then turned back. "Oh, and one other thing. If your ex is holding on to money for Skele, the man's going to come looking for it. And I wouldn't want to be the one there when he does." Stockton slid a business card on the counter and turned to walk out the door. "Call me if you change your mind and want to talk."

The door closed behind him, leaving the shop silent, except for the roaring in her ears.

Arms dealers. Money laundering. Prison time, Keely thought, staring blindly at the workbench before her. What in the name of God had Bradley done?

When the door opened to admit a trio of customers, she gave them an automatic smile and prayed that they wouldn't need anything, because she just didn't think she could cope just then.

The front door jingled again. "Hi, Keely."

Keely glanced up to see Lydia sailing in.

"Sorry I'm late." The redhead hurried to put her purse away. "Melly threw up all over herself and I had to change her for the babysitter. Roy's working late," she explained, tying on an apron.

"I have to go out for a minute," Keely said distractedly, neither noticing nor caring about the perplexed glance Lydia gave her. Air. She needed air. If she stayed in the shop one more minute she was going to suffocate.

Or start screaming and never stop.

She was out on the sidewalk before she knew it, not registering the cold, not hearing the greetings. She just let herself be carried along with the others who were drifting toward the common, laughing and joking, without a care in the world.

A week before, she'd been like them, happily moving through her days. Whatever fleeting unhappiness she'd felt over Bradley seemed a trifle, in retrospect. What she'd had seemed an idyllic existence.

Even if it had been a lie.

It was almost dizzying, Keely thought as she took a breath. How could Bradley have done it? Stealing was bad enough, but he'd begun dealing with bottom feeders. *Dangerous* bottom feeders. *If your ex is holding on to money for Skele, the man's going to come looking for it. And I wouldn't want to be the one there when he does.*

Her chest tightened and she inhaled again. Across the common, the garlanded Christmas tree rose from the snow-covered ground. Disgrace and legal problems were one thing. Physical threats were another. She'd never thought Bradley would take chances with true criminals. She never in a million years would have guessed that he'd embroil her and his mother.

What if the money was still out there? What if the dealer did come looking, and she had no better answers for him than for the police? She doubted "I don't know" would carry much weight with a killer.

She tried to take a breath but it seemed as though all oxygen had been sucked out of the air. The gay sounds of Christmas carols seemed to come from very far away. For a moment she stopped, swaying, gasping helplessly. Spots danced before her eyes.

"Sit," a voice ordered from behind her. Hands came down on her shoulders and eased her onto the wrought iron bench behind her. "Put your head between your knees and cup your hands together over your mouth."

"But—"

"Just do it."

Keely obeyed. Slowly, her breathing deepened. The terrifying breathlessness abated. After a few minutes, she stirred.

"Easy. Take it slow," the voice said. Lex's voice. When she straightened, he was sitting beside her. "Better now?"

She nodded and smiled wanly. "Yes, thank you."

"You were hyperventilating. What's going on? You look like you've seen a ghost."

"Not a ghost. I—"

Lex stared. "What the hell are you doing out here in just shirtsleeves?" he interrupted.

"I didn't think about it," she said vaguely, realizing all of a sudden that she was freezing.

He stripped off his jacket and put it around her shoulders. "You're nuts. Let's get you inside."

"I'm fine," she muttered.

"You're turning purple. Although I suppose it's better than sheet white, the way you were a little while ago."

She swallowed. "I had some bad news."

"Tell me," he said.

She never expected him to be nice. He sat next to her, solid and strong. She could feel the heat from his leg next to hers. Somehow, it made it easier to talk. "It's about Bradley. The federal agent just stopped by. John Stockton. They think Bradley..."

"What?"

She shook her head. It was so impossible to believe. "They think Bradley was laundering money for an arms dealer," she finished in a rush.

"An arms dealer?" Lex repeated incredulously.

"I know. I can't believe it, either, but Stockton says they've got proof. Bradley gambled himself into a hole and went to a loan shark. After your father died, he started embezzling from the company and laundering the money. And then he met the arms dealer."

"Great. Now he's in the laundry business. How much did he wash?" Lex asked.

"Two hundred million, they think."

He whistled. "Five or ten percent of that would be a nice chunk of change. Enough to pay off most of what he took from the company. Or to stay gone for a good long time."

Which would eliminate her main hope of exoneration. Keely rose and began to walk blindly toward a small stand of birches, Lex following. "I don't know what to do. Everything's just coming at me at once. And every time I turn around, it just gets worse."

Across the common, people were gathered about the tree, listening to the elementary-school chorus sing about decking the halls. They weren't worried about their lives falling apart. They weren't worried about being in danger. They were safe, content, the way she had been. She swung around to face Lex. "Did you mean it about working together?" she demanded.

He didn't answer right away. The lights around the edge of the common threw his cheekbones into sharp relief and gilded the tips of his lashes. "I don't know. You didn't seem to think it was such a good idea earlier today."

A smuggler, Bradley had told her. He had that rough, slightly lawless look that made it believable. A man who took what he wanted, did what he wanted, regardless of the rules. Her pulse began to speed up. "I've changed my mind."

"You're desperate."

"Does it matter?"

He didn't answer. He stepped closer, close enough that the white puffs of their breaths mingled. Around them, tiny white lights flickered in the birches, like fireflies. Out by the tree, there was a burst of applause. The chorus swung into "Merry Christmas, Baby."

It didn't make sense and Lex knew it. Sure, if she'd been any other woman, he'd have kissed her without a thought. Hell, who was he kidding? If she'd been any other woman they'd have long since been past kissing and onto finding out just what they could do for each other in bed. She wasn't just any woman, though. There was more at stake here than just satisfying his curiosity. A smart man would steer clear.

And even as he thought it, he found himself pulling her into his arms.

She was surprised at first, pliant against him, her lips parted so that he could feel the breath shuddering out. He tried to be gentle, God help him. But he could feel her move in the beginnings of response, he could taste her.

So he let himself savor that soft mouth of hers, the secret flavors beyond, feeling her slight curves beneath his jacket.

It only made him want more.

With a nip of teeth, a slick of tongue he tempted them both. When her head fell back, allowing him access to the soft underside of her jaw, he moved to the milk pale column of her throat, feeling the mad beat of her pulse against his lips. Beneath the cool facade was a real woman, silky and warm. The soft catch of her breath had him tightening.

He wanted way too much to be kissing like this out in the open. It had been an experiment, but he had to stop. There was too much impatience, too much hunger built up. If he didn't watch it, he'd take it too far. They were in public, he reminded himself. Time to stop. But he couldn't prevent himself from taking one more taste, and one more. And one more.

And then her arms came up around him and she turned avid and eager and wanting in his arms and he wasn't thinking about ending it anymore.

He wasn't thinking about anything but her.

They didn't feel the cool of the air. They didn't hear the strains of "Holly Jolly Christmas," soft notes of the woodwinds floating sweet and quiet through the night. There was just the slide of lip against lip, the stroke of fingers against hair, the suppressed sounds of hunger.

There was only two.

If he'd asked, Keely would have said no, but he hadn't asked. He'd taken. And it intoxicated her as nothing else ever had. The demand in his touch, the urgency in his taste had her pressing against him, fighting for more, more.

His hands slipped inside the jacket, sliding over her. And that mouth, that dangerous, delicious mouth was clever and persuasive against hers. She wanted more and she found herself taking, shifting her head to find a new angle, pressing against him to better feel his touch. Now, it was she who was impatient, she who demanded.

She who was standing at the doorway to a whole new world she'd never dreamed of.

Behind them, there was a collective gasp as the tree was switched on, as though the entire town had inhaled at once.

The entire town.

They jolted apart turning to stare at the source of the noise, and the applause that followed. A hundred yards away, the tree blazed with color. The figures of the townspeople were silhouetted against the light. Only here in the little grove was it dim and quiet.

Shaken, Keely stared at Lex. The adrenaline, the energy, still ricocheted through her system. Her lips still felt like they were vibrating with sensation. She didn't know where the hunger had billowed up from, only that it was nothing like anything she'd ever experienced with Bradley or any other man.

But this wasn't Bradley or any other man, this was Lex, the brother most likely to be arrested, who had had her twisting and clawing at him like a wanton. If there was any man in the world she had less business kissing in the dark, she couldn't come up with one offhand. And she had zero desire to think about the fact that he'd taken her so far with just a kiss.

"I must be out of my mind," she muttered, and without another look, began striding back toward the shop.

"Keely, wait a minute. We have to talk." With a few quick strides he was beside her.

"Forget it. I've got to get back to work." And she didn't want to be around him for another minute or God knew what she'd do.

She began unbuttoning the coat, sliding it off her shoulders as she walked quickly along. "Here's your jacket."

"Keep it, you're freezing."

"No." Because wearing it was a bit too much like having his arms around her. She swung around to face him. "Look, you want to talk? I'll talk. I'm going to work with you because someone's going to go down for this arms-dealer thing. Stockton was almost salivating. If there's any chance we can find something by pooling our resources, then I've got to do it. But that's all I'm going to do with you, got it?"

Lex studied her as though he'd never seen her before. "You like laying down the law."

"And you're not big on rules. Well, deal with it, champ. Right now, all I want to focus on is clearing up this mess Bradley's left. Maybe we can help each other on that, but you've got to figure out what you want."

"I know what I want," he replied, his eyes unreadable. "When can you go through my mother's papers?"

"As soon as possible." So she could find the answers and get the hell away from him.

"Tomorrow morning?"

"Fine." She slapped his jacket into his hands. "I'll see you at nine."

Chapter Five

So maybe Keely had had reason to be annoyed and rattled, Lex thought. He'd been a little rattled himself. The fact was, sitting at the table with his morning coffee, he couldn't for the life of him say why he'd kissed her the night before. Every practical part of him had been against it. One minute he'd been listing for himself the reasons it didn't make sense, the next he'd had his mouth crushed to hers.

And he could still smell her scent.

In the space of seconds, Keely Stafford, Ms. Junior League, his brother's supposed collaborator, had managed to wipe away the memory of every other woman he'd ever wanted. Except that he was beginning to seriously doubt that she'd had anything to do with Bradley's criminial fiasco. And he was beginning to see that there was more to her than just the standard charity socialite package.

Damned if that didn't just serve to intrigue him more than ever.

She was right, they had other things to focus on just then. Bradley was still missing and the authorities were still on the hunt for fall guys. Getting in the middle of something at that particular time wasn't smart. He had no business pushing it further.

He wasn't all that sure it mattered. There was something between them, the kiss had shown him that much. And he wasn't going to get her out of his head before he knew what it was.

The tap of high heels on the floor heralded Olivia's arrival. She wore a red suit with gold at her ears and her neck. There was no such thing as casual Saturday in Olivia's world.

"You're up early," she said as she poured herself some tea.

"The early bird catches the worm." Or the front-page photograph, anyway. Sleep was a luxury for guys like him. The news photographer who slept was the photographer who missed the shot.

Olivia looked amused. "You don't have to eat worms for breakfast. I'm sure Corinne can make you some eggs."

"I'm good," he said, taking another glance at the front news section. Bad crop on the shot of the aftermath of the Baghdad market bombing, he thought reflexively, then glanced closer to recognize the name on the byline. Poor Odenthal. He always did have rough luck when it came to the art department. But then, most photographers did. Too bad the wire service couldn't get a desk editor who could do the job right.

It was only after Lex had moved on to the next story that he registered the fact that he'd just looked at a shot of a place he'd been, a story he'd covered.

And thought about the desk editor.

Every other time he'd been back to the States for a break, seeing photographs in the paper had had just one effect—it had made him itch to be back out in the field. The field was what he was about. The story was what he was about, not the niceties of distributing photos for print.

He slapped the paper down and knocked back the rest of his coffee. It didn't mean anything except that he was burned out and maybe the few weeks downtime he was getting from the Bradley fiasco were a good thing.

"Everything all right?"

He glanced up to see Olivia watching him. "Yeah, sure, fine. I should probably go take a look at your office to get myself oriented. Keely's going to be here soon." He saw Olivia's lips tighten. "Is it going to be a problem?" he asked. It might just be for him, if he couldn't get that damned kiss out of his head.

"I told you last night, I'm holding a committee meeting for the Christmas gala this morning, so I won't be there when you're looking through things. Remember, these are my personal finances. Be sure you keep an eye on her."

That, he could guarantee.

"I'm not comfortable having her paw through my private papers," Olivia added after a moment.

"Well, you'd better get comfortable. Right now, she's about the only hope you've got."

She took a sip of tea. "And you really think there's a chance she had nothing to do with this scheme?"

"I don't know. I'm beginning to think she's in the clear." He remembered the look on Keely's face the night before, the distress as she'd told him about the arms dealer. "Anyway, you know what they say, keep you friends close and your enemies closer."

Olivia flushed and set her cup down, centering it carefully in the saucer. "It's so hard to think Bradley could have done something like this."

"I know. But all the facts point to it. He's gone. We haven't heard a word from him. That should tell you something right there. He wasn't just taking money for himself. He was laundering money for—"

"Stop." She covered her ears. "I know this is all important but I can't listen to it right now."

"You want me to just leave it alone?" Lex asked incredulously.

"No. I want you to look into it. I just…I just can't hear the details. Please." She bit her lip. "He's my son. I can't help loving him."

"Good. He'll need it if they ever find him. But in the meantime we need to get you off the hook, and maybe Keely can help with that. So are you going to play nice when she comes over?"

Olivia recovered enough to give him a starchy look. "Have you ever seen me be anything other than polite?"

"I've seen you give people frostbite," he said neutrally.

The corners of her mouth twitched. "You should give your mother more respect."

"I give my mother a world of respect. But I've gotta warn you, I think she could take you down."

Olivia snorted. "Now, that I'd like to see."

"She used to have a mean tennis backhand."

"Experience trumps strength anytime." She accepted toast from the maid. "By the way, I got a call from Bill Hartley yesterday. The chairman of the board," she elaborated.

"The Alexander board?"

"Of course. He wants to know when we're going to fill the open spot."

Lex watched the maid refill his coffee from the sideboard. "At the risk of asking the obvious, what open spot?"

"Bradley's, of course." Olivia's voice was brisk. "They removed him as soon as the scandal broke. Now they need to bring someone else on."

"Why are they coming to you?"

She gave him a surprised glance as she spread marmalade on her toast. "Why, I'm the primary shareholder. I thought you knew."

"Dad took the company public, what, three years after I left? I figured you guys kept a stake but that's about it. They don't carry a lot of financial papers the places I hang out."

"When your father took the company public, he kept fifty-one percent for us and gave Bradley ten," she said reprovingly and took a bite of her toast.

Lex raised a brow. "That's a lot of stock right off the top."

"He wanted to be sure the family retained control and we have. Whomever we want on the board goes on the board. While he was alive, Pierce was chairman."

No big surprise there. "Did Bradley step in after he died?"

Olivia shook her head. "The board didn't think he had enough experience." She hesitated. "I didn't, either."

"Good call. He managed to do plenty of damage as COO."

"Notwithstanding which we've now got a board with an open position, an even number of members and some key votes coming up. We need to have the full complement."

Lex shrugged. "Let Hartley and his buddies come up with some candidates. I'm sure they have ideas."

"I suppose." Then a pause. "You could throw your name in the hat for the board position," she added casually.

He stared at her. "I'm the one who's been living in Third World countries and war zones for the past decade, remember? Forget it. I'm not your guy."

"I think we can decide who our guy is."

"Thanks but no thanks. I'd be—" He broke off at the low tones of the doorbell. "I guess this is Keely," he said with relief.

"Don't think you're off the hook about this," Olivia warned as he headed toward the front door.

Like hell he wasn't. He'd get Olivia cleared of the money-laundering charges and then he'd head back to his real life.

And try not to think too much about Keely Stafford.

One thing Keely could say for the kiss—it almost made her look forward to having Olivia Alexander around as a buffer when they looked through her home office. And that was saying something. Keely had been anticipating dealing with Olivia with about as much enthusiasm as she would a root canal. All things considered, though, it was a good way to diffuse the tension between her and Lex.

Because tension there would be.

Unconsciously, she raised her fingertips to her lips. Relax, she told herself as she stood on the front steps of the Alexander home, trying to ignore the nerves fluttering in her stomach. It had taken her a long time to fall asleep the night before. While she'd been at the shop, she'd kept herself busy. When she'd made it home after closing up, her parents had been there to give her the full account of their party. But once she'd been in bed, clad only in a cotton sleep shirt, the flashbacks kept unspooling themselves over and over: Lex moving forward, leaning in to kiss her, the instant she'd felt his lips on hers.

And the moment she'd lost control.

It had been like something had taken her over. Or someone. And that was the last thing, the very last thing she needed just then. She didn't want anyone else taking control of her. She had a flashing memory of Bradley and his woman, the frenzied movement, the cries. Keely had almost handed her life over to him and he'd very nearly destroyed it. The last thing she was ready to do now was give someone else a chance.

Especially a man who didn't believe in playing by the rules.

A sudden click startled her and the door opened to reveal the maid.

And behind her stood Lex.

The nerves Keely thought she'd tamped down billowed up. He was clean-shaven this time; it only served to make him more appealing in jeans and charcoal V-neck. The pine-colored T-shirt beneath brought out the green in his eyes.

Eyes that gazed at her with a hint of speculation. "Morning."

"Good morning," she said as the maid took her jacket away. It left her feeling oddly naked in her jeans and sweater, as though she were being stripped as an offering for a potentate.

"I wasn't sure you'd show," Lex said.

She hadn't been sure, either, that morning, but there was too much at stake not to. "I told you I'd be here."

"So you did."

To avoid looking at him, she glanced around the entryway and the reception rooms beyond. She'd been there before, of course, with Bradley, but it was hard not to be impressed with the Alexanders' Italian Revival mansion. Because a mansion, frankly, it was, all intricate moldings and ornate ceilings and cavernous rooms. How Olivia managed to live there all alone without going mad, Keely couldn't say. Perhaps that was why she'd always pushed Bradley to visit.

As if in time with Keely's thoughts, Olivia came around the corner. "Keely," she said coolly, "what a pleasure to have you here."

Considering the circumstances, it was a somewhat strange greeting, but Keely would go with it. She put her hand out to clasp Olivia's. "It's always nice to see you."

"Would you like some coffee or tea? Toast?" Olivia gestured toward the breakfast table.

"No, thank you," Keely said. "I'm fine."

"Perhaps later. How are your parents?"

"Fine, thanks." And how is your missing criminal of a son? Olivia was acting for all the world like Keely had dropped by on a social call.

"Please give them my holiday wishes. Who knows if I'll see them? Everything's so hectic this time of year."

"Yes, well, the holidays are always that way," Keely found herself saying lamely.

Lex coughed, a faint suggestion of amusement hovering around the corners of his mouth.

Keely threw him a scowl.

"I suppose you're right," Olivia went on. "Would you like to sit down?"

"Actually, I'd rather get started." Maybe it wasn't her place, but continuing the excruciatingly polite exchange while Lex stood watching was stretching Keely's nerves to the breaking point. The sooner she could be done with it all and away from him, the better.

"Very well," Olivia said. "As I told Lex, the DAR Christmas gala committee is meeting here in just a few minutes, but I can at least show you where everything is. If you'll just follow me…" Heels tapping, she headed down the hallway.

Lex had expected Olivia to lead them into the pale office that held her fussy inlaid rosewood desk and her Aubusson rugs. Instead, she walked right past and swung open the door to Pierce's old study. Lex stepped through the doorway and stepped back in time.

It was the one room in the house that had stayed the same: forest green walls, coffered ceiling, dark wood bookshelves with leather-bound books, solid mahogany desk that had stood in the same corner for generations. The polished brass desk lamp was the same, the walnut and gold pen-and-pencil set, even the blue-green art glass bowl. Perhaps it was a little less rigorously neat than he recalled, but it was otherwise the same.

"Since when did Dad start keeping paperclips in this?" Lex asked, fingering the bowl.

"Never. I think Bradley just started tossing things in there. I gave up emptying it after a while." She turned to Keely and hesitated. "This was my husband's office. Bradley used it when he was here, as I think you know. And the computer. Any records that are still left after the search are in the files."

"What did they take?" Lex asked.

"Not much, really. They apparently already had access to my phone and bank records." Her mouth tightened. "They poked around, mostly. They wanted to take my mobile phone, of all things, on the grounds that it might have incriminating text messages on it. Text messages. I ask you," she said in indignation. "I'm not some teenager."

Lex fought back a smile. "They were probably worried about something Bradley might have left on it."

"Even so," she said.

"The computer's still here, though."

"Oh, yes. They originally wanted to take it but the judge who issued the warrant wouldn't approve." Her voice was smug as she unlocked the desk.

It was the latest model laptop, its sleek metallic blue case out of place in the traditional surroundings. When

Keely pressed the power button, it swung into operation with a hum.

"It's not likely that we'll find anything the investigators didn't but we should still look," Keely said.

"What can we hope to find that they haven't? They can subpoena anything they want." There was a tinge of hopelessness in Olivia's voice.

"They don't know Bradley like we do. They don't know how he thinks. And they're not infallible. They could have missed something. We have to check every possibility." Keely's fingers tapped on the keys. "Speaking of which, we should pull a credit report on you, just to be sure there aren't any surprises. I'll write down the number and either you or Lex can order them. All you need is your social-security number."

Lex walked over to the bookshelves and began pulling volumes out at random. "So what did Bradley spend his time doing when he was in here?" He glanced over his shoulder to Olivia.

"Oh, this and that. He paid bills, reviewed my bank statements and brokerage accounts. If he came on a Friday, he'd make calls. Usually those times he brought his own laptop so he could e-mail. We've got town Wi-Fi here now," she added. "It was nice having him here. It was like when Pierce—" Her voice caught. A second went by and she shook her head. "I'm sorry, I just need to… Look around all you like. I'll be next door, preparing for my meeting." She opened the connecting door between the two offices.

"Mom—" Lex took two steps after her.

"I'll be fine," she said without turning. The doorbell bonged. "The committee's arriving. I have to get ready."

Lex threw a helpless look at Keely. "Stay," she mouthed to him.

"Sorry," he said softly as he came back over to the desk. "She's having a tough time with this."

"Anyone would," Keely said.

He pulled up a chair and sat next to her, far too close for her peace of mind. "I can search drawers and files. I just need to know what you're looking for."

A clear head, Keely told herself. "Something to prove that neither Olivia or I knew about the LLCs, that he put us on the boards without our permission or knowledge. Any files or contacts that might be part of starting up the LLCs would help, any contacts with his Latvian friend or whatever lawyer he worked with."

"I'll check the drawers." Lex rose and pushed the chair out of the way. "What about e-mail or notes?" he asked from beside her.

"You go into business with a piranha, you keep records to protect yourself. Particularly Bradley. He's always been one to cover his ass."

"He's too smart to keep something like that in his condo," she said thoughtfully.

"Exactly. He considered this his office away from home. It stands to reason he might have squirreled it away somewhere here. He'd have known that even a search couldn't be too comprehensive if my mother wasn't a primary suspect." Lex pulled out one drawer after another and inspected the backs and undersides.

"Of course, your mother or the maid could stumble over it at anytime, depending on what it is. Do you think he'd risk that?"

"What's the risk?" Lex slid in the last drawer. "My

mother left all the financial dealings to him and the maid wouldn't pay any attention to business papers."

"He could have a hidey hole somewhere else, though." Keely gave him a sudden, quick glance. "What about the room he used when he stayed here? Do you know if they searched that?"

From the hallway came the murmurs of arriving DAR members.

"It can't hurt to look, whether they did or not," Lex said. He stood in one fluid motion just as Keely pushed back the chair and rose.

Only to find herself almost lip to lip with him.

For an instant, every thought in her head scattered. Neither she nor Lex moved. Out in the hall, they could hear the clinks of teacups and spoons from the garden room at the back. Inside, humming tension filled the room.

Then Lex inclined his head a fraction and stepped away.

It was nothing, Keely told herself fiercely as she followed him into the hallway. It was just being uncomfortably close to someone she didn't know very well, no more than that. It was nothing like that…whatever it was she'd felt the night before. Nothing at all.

Lex stopped at the bottom of the stairs and nodded for her to go ahead of him. "Ladies first."

She shook her head. "No, you. Please."

"Come on, with my mother and half the DAR in the other room?" he asked. "They'll sense it somehow and come out and string me up for bad manners. No chance. You go."

During the two years she and Bradley had been engaged, Keely had never seen the upstairs of the Alexander home. Though she'd been curious, definitely curious. The few times the two of them had been in Chilton together, she'd stayed with her parents and he with his. It didn't matter that they were going to be married; that was just the way it was done. Climbing the stairs now, Keely felt as though she were sneaking into the inner sanctum.

And she couldn't help but be aware of Lex just behind her. She could hear his breath, hear the slide of his hand on the carved oak banister, the tread of his feet on the stair runner beneath their feet. She found herself hyper-conscious of her every motion, wondering if he was watching.

Knowing, somehow, that he was.

At the top step, she breathed a silent sigh of relief and stepped back to give Lex an inquiring look.

"Go on," he said.

"Where?"

"Bradley's room."

She shrugged. "I don't know where it is. I've never been up here before."

"You haven't…?" He gave a wry smile of understanding. "You wouldn't have, I guess. My mother's pretty old school. It's down here."

Bradley's walls were painted in a deep, luxurious teal. Olivia had redecorated it a year or so before, Keely recalled. It must have been per Bradley's request because there was none of Olivia's fondness for the traditional. There was also no personality to the room. Zip. None. It didn't look a bit like his condo in Manhattan. It might have been a room in a stylish boutique hotel. There was a black framed full-length mirror leaning against the wall, a narrow desk, a chrome and frosted glass bedside table.

And a bed.

Keely felt instantly awkward. It was as though they were intruding—not on Bradley, because there was nothing of him here, but on someone. And that bed, that enormous bed, practically the only thing in the room so that it was almost impossible not to stare at it. Would the atmosphere have felt so…charged if she'd been standing there with any man? Or was it because she was standing there with Lex?

And why the hell was it that when she was here searching the past in order to save her future, she couldn't stop thinking about his mouth on hers, his hands running down her body, the sharp male scent of him, the heat of his breath as he—

Stop it.

No distractions. This certainly was no time to get thinking about aberrations like the night before. It had been a lapse, she reminded herself impatiently, a mistake. Nothing more.

"Where do you want to start?" Lex asked.

Keely jumped. "The bed. I mean, you. Search the bed, that is," she fumbled. "Check behind the headboard and underneath. I think it's got some built-in drawers. I'll check the closet."

And that was where she fled.

It would be possible to sound more idiotic, she supposed, but it would take some doing. Where was that poise that she was always able to summon up at work? This was its own kind of job, a crucial job, so why was she babbling like some bubble-headed bimbo?

Keely opened the door to the walk-in closet to find built in bureaus, which at least answered the question of why the room was so bare. And gave her something to do. She began pulling out drawers. The search was unlikely to yield any clues but it was worth it to be sure.

At least there wasn't much to search. Bradley hadn't spent all that much time in Chilton. There were a few shirts and pairs of jeans, a couple of sweaters, a single suit. A couple of the baseball hats he liked to wear sailing. Add T-shirts and shoes and underclothes, and that was pretty well it.

The things on the shelf that ran above the clothes racks were the sole items that spoke of a life prior to the present day. She found a lacrosse racket and helmet, a pair of downhill skis and poles. And at the very end, all the way inside, a tennis racket.

For a minute, she just held it in her hands, staring down at it. They had been magic, those long-ago days on the courts. There had been a time Bradley had been her knight in shining armor. And even once the shine on the armor had dulled, she'd liked him well enough. Respected him, even. Feeling they weren't right together hadn't changed that.

She would never in a million years have guessed that behind the Bradley she knew, the Bradley she'd practically lived with for more than two years, was a completely different person. A corrupt, careless person. If she'd been that wrong about him, what did it mean about everybody else? What did it mean about her?

What did that mean about Lex?

She heard a sound behind her and he was there, filling the doorway of the closet.

"Need some help in here?" he asked.

Adrenaline surged through her veins. The light shining down from overhead cast his eyes into shadow. This wasn't the town common. They weren't in public now but in this private place. Her heart thudded. Anticipation? Alarm? She couldn't say, only that she couldn't have moved if her life depended on it.

Lex reached toward her and she stood, motionless.

He pulled the chain above her head and with a click the overhead light turned off.

"Maybe we should go downstairs," he said, his face was scrupulously wiped of expression. "I think we've done everything we can do here."

After Bradley's room and the closet, being with Lex in the office downstairs felt positively relaxing. The door was open, there were people around. There could be no repeat of those uncomfortable moments of intimacy.

And if she could just forget about them, everything would be fine.

Lex turned from the last of the bookshelves, having gone through each and every book. "We're done here."

"Did you check the backs and undersides of the bookcase?" Keely asked.

He snorted. "They're six feet high and solid walnut. I doubt he could move one even without the books in it, assuming my mother and the maid were ever gone long enough for him to get that far."

There was the tap of heels and Olivia walked in. "What about me being gone long enough?"

"Bradley, hiding things on the backs of the shelves."

"Oh, those things weigh a ton. They've never been moved since I've been here." She glanced at Lex and Keely hopefully. "Any luck?"

"Not so far," Lex said, "although we know where it's not."

"Well, the committee is gone, so let me know what you need."

Lex pointed to the tall oak filing cabinet. "You can find us the key for that so I can search it," he said.

"Oh, of course. I should have given you the key before I left. I've been locking it lately when I'm not using it. The help, you know," she elaborated.

What would it be like to live with someone you couldn't trust? Keely wondered. Walking around locking things, worrying, never having any privacy. Like being a prisoner in your own house.

She watched as Olivia came back out of her office with a small, gold-toned key and handed it to Lex. He tried to slide it into the lock but it stuck. "Are you sure this is the right key?"

"Of course it is. I use it all the time. It's just a little sticky."

"A little? You ever heard of powdered graphite?"

Olivia frowned. "What's that?"

"Stuff that you use to keep a lock from being like this."

"Oh, it just takes a little finessing," she said impatiently, holding her hand out for the key.

Lex dropped it into her hand, holding it by the keychain, a little yellow plastic cutout of a house with Chilton Realty printed on it. He laughed. "Chilton Realty. Good old Eva Jo Romano. Is she still sending you pads of paper and keychains?"

"Oh, she finally gave up on us." Olivia fiddled with the key. "Bradley started looking for a place around here a couple of years ago, though, and it started her back up."

She didn't notice that both Lex and Keely stiffened.

"Bradley started looking for a place?" Keely repeated carefully.

"A house. He wanted it for the two of you to use once you were married. So you could stay together. I told him you could stay here but he didn't listen." The lock went over with a snap and she glanced up triumphantly.

Only to see them both staring at her.

"What?" she asked.

"Bradley bought a house," Lex said.

Olivia waved it away. "No, he just looked. Said he couldn't find anything that was right."

"That doesn't mean he didn't get one without telling you." Lex was pacing around the room as he spoke.

"Are you thinking the same thing I'm thinking?" Keely asked him, an unholy excitement fluttering in her gut.

He nodded. "A safe house. If he worked it so it stayed off the record, he'd have that nice hidey hole you were talking about earlier."

"And if we find it, we might get all the proof we need." Even as Keely cautioned herself not to get her hopes up, the grin spread over her face.

"So what do we do now, call the real-estate agent?" Olivia asked, some of their excitement infecting her.

Keely shrugged. "I doubt she'll say anything to us. People are pretty gun shy when it comes to violating client privilege."

"Eva Jo? She's practically like a member of the family." Lex leaned against the desk. "Her face was always staring up at us from those telephone notepads she passed out. With a few additions, of course. Fangs, horns, missing teeth…"

Keely's lips twitched. "And I'm sure she felt close to you, too. That said, if she's not supposed to tell you, she's not going to tell you. Even if you did give her horns," she added. "Anyway, there's no guarantee he even went to her. He might have looked a little bit but if he wanted to buy the place incognito, he probably went to someone who didn't know him."

"Why? It won't be under his name. It'd probably be under one of the LLCs, wouldn't it?"

"Not necessarily. Safe means he'd want to keep it completely disconnected from any of the LLCs so it couldn't be traced back to him if everything went to hell. It could be under a fake name. It could be under Olivia's name. That could be where the millions went."

Lex stopped pacing and dropped back into his chair. "Wouldn't the feds know, if that were the case?"

"Maybe. Maybe not."

"So how do we check it out?"

Keely started shutting down the computer. "Look through all the files, first. If we don't find anything then Monday first thing we'll go down to the town hall and look through the property transfers, see if we can find anything."

"And if we do?"

"Then we figure out a way inside."

Chapter Six

"How can I help you?" The pretty young clerk at the town hall gave them a practiced smile.

Keely smiled back. "I want to look at property-transfer records for the past two—"

"We've got it all in the computer," the clerk interrupted, pointing to the terminals. "You just look it up by the name or address."

"What if you don't have the name or address?" Lex asked.

"I'm sorry?"

"We don't have the address."

The smile faded. She tapped a tidy, pink varnished nail on the glossy white counter. "You've got to have a name or address to use the computer."

"Exactly," Keely said, searching for patience. The

contents of the filing cabinet had been a bust. "We don't have either, so how can we look up transfers?"

The clerk gave them the frown and sigh reserved for people who refused to cooperate and ask the standard questions. "I don't see why you wouldn't have a name or address."

Lex leaned in and gave the clerk one of those smiles that could weaken the knees of any woman. Keely knew from personal experience. "Lynette?" he read off the clerk's badge.

"That's right." Her voice suddenly sounded oddly breathless.

"Pretty name. Listen, Lynette, is there somewhere we can just look at a list of all real-estate transactions that happened in the past two years?"

"Well, we have the land record books in the basement," she told him, eager to please. "They're listed by alphabetical order."

"That's fine. They have all the transactions for the year, right?" Lex asked.

"Actually, they're in groups of ten years," Lynette chirped.

Keely's heart sank.

The ledger-sized books hit the long table with a thump. "Ladies and gentlemen, I give you the land record books for the first decade of the twenty-first century," Lex announced. "*A* through *L* and *M* through *Z.* What's your pleasure?"

"Funny," Keely said darkly and dragged the top book over in front of her. It was nearly the thickness of a telephone book, hundreds of pages, each of which would have to be combed through. The real-estate boom had made for busy times in land records.

They sat, not in a room but in an enormous fireproof vault in the basement of the Chilton Town Hall. The space could easily have accommodated a large dinner party. The air held the dry, bone-deep chill of a climate-controlled space. Overhead, a dying fluorescent light buzzed like an angry hornet, flickering out, only to flicker back on an instant later.

"*M*," Lex siad, and opened the ledger before him.

The ledgers were large and the type was eye-blurringly tiny, especially after a couple of hours of staring at it. Neither of them had thought to bring rulers or anything to help them keep their places. The worst part was that they hadn't a clue what they were looking for and only a faint hope they might find it.

Sixty seconds a page, three hundred and fifty some-odd pages in a book, two of them to cover the decade. "Who knew so much property turned over around here?" Keely muttered.

"They're an acquisitive bunch, these New Englanders," Lex said.

"Or indecisive, since they buy as much as they sell."

Sixty seconds a page, three hundred and fifty pages in a book, two of them to cover the decade. Minute ticked into minute. One hour crept into two, two slid into three and Keely found herself at the bottom of a page of dense type with absolutely no recollection of what she'd seen.

She stopped and rolled her shoulders.

Lex glanced over. "I know. I keep getting to the bottom of a page and thinking I can't remember a single name I read."

He hadn't shaved that morning and his darkened jaw and battered leather jacket seemed utterly incongruous with the bookish task of reviewing the ledgers. Still, he'd come of his own volition and had been working without complaint since they'd arrived.

And if she'd found herself faintly distracted at having him sitting a foot away from her, she'd just have to deal with it.

"When in doubt, repeat," Keely said. "The worst thing would be to have it be there and miss it."

"Time for a break, then."

"Not yet. I want to finish. I'm so close to the end of this book."

"It won't do you any good if you space out and skip something."

"I don't space out," she grumbled.

"Far be it from me to suggest it." Lex rubbed his eyes. "You know," he added, "we're assuming he bought here. What if he bought somewhere else?"

Keely looked at him in horror. "Perish the thought. Anyway, it doesn't make sense that he'd go somewhere else. He needed someplace easy to get to, someplace he had a plausible reason to visit regularly without arousing suspicion. Chilton is perfect. All he had to do when he was visiting was nip out and stop by on his way to see a friend or go to the store or whatever."

"Assuming nobody saw him come and go."

She sighed and started again at the top of the page. "Keep looking," she ordered.

"Anybody ever tell you you're bossy?" Lex asked mildly.

"It's for the greater good."

"That's me, all about the greater good."

"I'm so glad to hear it."

"Even if I do wind up blind because of it."

"Uh-huh," she said absently, back to scanning lists of names.

Silence fell again, broken only by the rustle of turning pages and sound of their breath. Sixty seconds a page, three hundred and fifty pages in a book, two of them to cover the decade. Three hours crept into four, four hours slid into…

"Holy crap," Lex said explosively.

Keely jumped. "What? What did you find? Bradley's name? Your mother's?"

"No," he said. "I found yours."

The road was narrow and winding. In colonial times, it had been a major thoroughfare and stone walls built laboriously by hand still rose on either side. More than two hundred and fifty years had changed things, though. It wasn't a major highway anymore. It wasn't even a county road. It was just a withered offshoot well outside of town that went nowhere.

In summer, with the trees leafed out, it would be green and shady and lovely, Keely thought. Now, in the waning weeks of the year, it was a study in black and gray and dirty white.

"We're lucky most of the snow has gone from the nor'easter," she commented as Lex's rental Jeep bounced over the ruts. "It doesn't look like the plows made it up this far."

"That's probably part of what made him pick the place." Lex seemed at home fighting to keep the vehicle on the narrow ribbon of dirt and eroding asphalt. "It's a good way to discourage unwelcome guests."

They missed it the first time around, forcing Lex to reverse to find the little lane that led to the pale gray house hidden among the trees. At least the builder had thought to put in a horseshoe driveway so that it would be easy to get back to the road. They drove up to the front and stopped.

"What if Bradley's here?" Keely asked suddenly. In the first shock of finding the listing and tracking down the property, it hadn't occurred to her. Now, though...

"If he's here then we've found him and our problem's solved."

"Only if he suddenly decides to cooperate."

"You might be surprised." Lex turned off the engine. "I don't imagine living on the run is all it's cracked up to be. And even if he doesn't want to cooperate, he's still cornered."

"Then again, cornered animals are the most dangerous."

"Are you calling your ex-fiancé an animal?" Lex asked in amusement as they got out.

That stopped her for a moment. "Well, I—"

He flicked her a grin. "Relax. Anyway, I don't think you have to worry. No car in the drive, no smoke from the chimney. I doubt he's here."

"You don't know that it's heated with a stove."

He pointed to a pile covered in bright blue plastic.

"Twenty bucks says that under that tarp is a cord of hard wood. And…" He knocked hard on the front door. Only silence greeted them. "Empty."

Keely glowered at him. "Do you get tired of always being right?" she demanded.

Lex grinned. "Never," he said. "Want to take a look around your house?"

Her house. It was a surprise but technically, she supposed, it was true. Her name was on the deed, as far as they could discover—even if she had zero idea where that deed actually was.

In a month of shocking incidents, few things had been as startling as the sight of her name, resting calmly in the ledger next to dozens of others. How Bradley had managed to do it without her knowledge, without her presence at signing, she had no idea. Then again, with enough money, a willing lawyer and a spare corporation—and God knew he had those—anything was apparently possible, as a mortgage broker had told them.

Including ending the day with a house she hadn't known existed, much less belonged to her.

And which was currently shut up tight. No great surprise there, nor was it a surprise to find all the drapes drawn. There was a rather spectacular picture window at the back that overlooked a clearing Keely imagined was gorgeous in summer.

"Do you think it's hooked up to town power and water?" she asked, picking her way through the slush as they walked around it.

Lex crunched along beside her, seeming far more comfortable prowling around what felt like someone else's property than she was. Then again, given his background, maybe he was more accustomed to it. "Power, maybe. Phone, cable. There was wiring strung along that sorry excuse for a road we were on. I'd put my money on well water and a generator, though." He pointed to the gray metal box hulking up next to one side of the house. "A place like this, you never know when the power's going to go out. It pays to be prepared."

She pulled up the doormat.

Lex gave her a sidelong glance. "You really think you're going to find a key?"

"No. But wouldn't we feel like idiots if it was there and we didn't check?"

"I guess you've got a point."

She dropped the mat back down. "Nothing here." She glanced at Lex. "Under a rock?"

"A fake one, maybe. Or it could be stuck under a flowerpot somewhere."

Or hung on a nail on a fencepost or in the porch light or even on a lintel. They searched all those locations and more without success. Half an hour later, standing in the flower beds beside the raised deck, Lex turned to her.

"Any more ideas?"

"Maybe there's not a key to find," Keely said thoughtfully. "Maybe he carries it with him."

Lex shook his head. "If we're right and he's got the goods in there, he's not going to want to have anything on him that would tie him to the place. Including the key. It'll be somewhere else, somewhere safe."

"Such as?"

He shrugged. "Not his condo. Maybe your apartment?"

"If it was there, the cops found it."

"Not necessarily. They can't just come into your house and take whatever they see. It has to be called out on the search warrant," he said. She wasn't going to ask how he knew. "To add on a key, they would have had to have known about the house and there wasn't a word about it. So wherever it is, there's a pretty good chance it's still there."

"But not here."

"No," he agreed.

She put her hands on her hips and surveyed the back face of the house doubtfully. "We could break a window."

"No way. There could be security. He could have someone watching the place for him. The last thing we want is for the cops to show up or for Bradley to find out what's going on."

"You're probably right."

"And it's winter," he continued. "You break a window, you're letting in rain, snow, bugs, small furry animals, large furry animals… Not to mention large hairless animals, also known as teenagers."

"All right, already. It was just an idea." And he'd surprised her yet again. Not that smuggling meant he was accustomed to B&E but she'd always assumed that breaking one set of laws tended to make a person cavalier about the others.

"It wasn't a bad idea," Lex said. "It would have gotten us inside."

"Inside doesn't sound like such a bad idea." Keely shivered. "I don't suppose you know how to pick a lock, do you?"

Shadows loomed over them in the chilling afternoon. Lex glanced up at her from where he'd been picking up rocks, and straightened. There was something rough and reckless and all too compelling about him. She shivered again, but this time from something other than temperature.

He squinted at her blue leather peacoat. "When are you going to start dressing for the cold? You grew up here. You know what December means."

"I'm wearing a sweater and a jacket. That should be enough."

He flicked at the open front of her coat. "It is if you button it up."

"Anyway," she continued, ignoring him, "it's not like you're one to talk. What is that, a flannel shirt and a bomber jacket? You're wearing less than I am."

"I'm wearing layers." He flipped aside the collar of the flannel shirt to show the Henley beneath. "And I'm used to being uncomfortable."

Used to being uncomfortable, used to hanging around the scratchy parts of the world. "So are you really a smuggler?" she blurted.

"What?" He stared at her.

"Bradley told me you were a smuggler. He said you worked the black market and that was why you went to all the strange places you do." Rough, capable, slightly dangerous looking—if he'd been an actor, they'd have cast him for the role.

Lex gave a short laugh and flung the small stone he held into the woods. "Man, he tagged all the bases, didn't he?"

"What does that mean?"

"How many other people do you think he fed that line of bull? It would explain a lot."

"I take it you're not a smuggler?"

Lex snorted. "I sold my second pair of jeans one time when I was in China and broke. I think I was all of twenty. Does that count?"

"What are you doing in all those places, then?"

"Taking pictures. I'm a photographer."

Bradley had just laughed at the photography story. Then again, Bradley had lied and cheated and stolen… "Bradley said you just used that for a cover story."

Lex didn't answer, just made a derisive noise.

She shook her head. "I don't understand it. Why lie about everything?"

"You got me. These days it doesn't sound like he needs a reason, just an opportunity." He shrugged and bent to check another rock, his dark hair falling over his forehead. "Brad and I aren't exactly close. We don't see things the same way."

There was a time when she'd have been sure what that meant. There was a time it had been simple: Bradley was the good brother, Trey—Lex—was the bad one. Only Bradley hadn't turned out to be so good after all, and Lex was here at her side, helping her out of trouble, making her laugh, looking at her now with those green, green eyes that sent something skittering madly about her stomach, and suddenly she wasn't thinking any more about Bradley and the trouble she was in. Suddenly all she could think about was Lex's mouth and his hands and what it would be like to kiss him again.

He straightened slowly, his eyes darkening in the

growing dusk. He didn't say anything and neither did she. All she could do was watch, mesmerized, as he took one step toward her, then another, then another.

Somewhere deep inside her, the distant drumbeat of desire began to thud. This was foolish, it was a mistake, an anxious voice protested in her head. She'd been so wrong about Bradley, who was to say she wasn't just as wrong about Lex? The voice was drowned out by the roaring in her ears, though. By the beat of her heart.

Maybe it was a risk but she couldn't really stop long enough to care. Somehow, she couldn't make it matter. Somehow, all she could do was want.

And when his mouth covered hers, all she could do was glory in it.

It wasn't a surprise, this time. She knew it was happening and yet it took her breath away all the same. Some far off part of her registered alarm but it was hard to take it too seriously when the warmth of his mouth was on hers.

Because it was warm. It was December, there was snow on the ground, but his lips heated hers like he was connected to some inner furnace. And through some alchemy of desire, the heat became need, spreading through her body, soaking into her bones. Yet all the while he was barely touching her, teasing with featherlight touches of his lips and quick, tempting flicks of his tongue until she heard her own helpless moan.

Until she was impatient for more.

How could just the hint of his taste seem so familiar? How could it make her crave? Keely's lips parted and she rested her open mouth against his so that just the tips of their tongues danced together, so that their breath mixed. If he could tease, she could tease, too, making them both wait, giving just enough to keep them both wanting.

This time it was Lex who made the impatient noise. And it was Lex who dragged them both deeper into a maelstrom of sensations and flavors that dizzied her. Suddenly it wasn't about teasing, it was about taking. It wasn't about desire but raw need. There was a flash of something, then, something elemental that lurked beneath the veneer of civilization and the rules of seduction. Something that could sweep her into a hot madness if she let it.

And it was that that had her pulling away, finally, breathing hard.

"Okay, now I really want to find that damned key," Lex muttered, his voice tight with frustration.

Keely dragged her fingers through her hair, feeling like a stranger to herself. "We've looked for it everywhere. We're pretty well at a stopping point now. Let's just go."

Lex swept her back into his arms. "I wouldn't call this a stopping point, darlin'," he murmured against her lips.

And she felt the treacherous desire flow through her again. It took all she had to resist it, all she had to press her hands against his chest. "No, okay? Enough."

He dropped his hands, staring at her with a flicker of temper. "Okay, what's going on? Now you're here, now you're gone? Don't even try to tell me that you weren't into it this time because I know better."

"I won't." There was no point in saying it hadn't been smart or they shouldn't do it because she'd known all that and she'd still wanted the kiss. She'd wanted him.

And he deserved some honesty.

Keely moistened her lips. "Look, life's been pretty… confusing lately. There's been a lot going on." And she was talking in circles. Honesty, she reminded herself. "Forget about the whole legal tangle. Bradley and I were engaged for two years and it ended, and it ended about as ugly as it could."

"What happened?" His voice was soft, his gaze attentive.

"It doesn't matter. What matters is that I get my feet back under me, and that's not going to happen if we take up where we left off, here." Her throat tightened. "I'm still trying to get over one Alexander. I don't need to go onto another."

"I'm not Bradley," he said.

"It doesn't matter. I just need some time, can you understand that?" She paced away and swung back to face him. "The last time I kissed an Alexander, it didn't turn out well. I'm not in a hurry to dive back in."

Lex opened his mouth to say something and then shut it.

"What?" Keely asked.

"Nothing." Long seconds went by while he stared at the ground, hands on his hips. Then he raised his head. "You're right," he repeated. "You're right. Come on, it's getting dark and it's supposed to snow tonight. Let's get out of here while we can see."

The ride back to Chilton was mostly silent, though not awkwardly so, Keely realized in surprise. Lex had an ability to let things be, it seemed, unlike Bradley. And she was grateful for it. She couldn't even understand herself, let alone explain what was going on to him.

When they crossed the outskirts of town, he stirred. "I'll take another look around my mom's house, see if I can find anything resembling a key."

"I should probably go in and give my apartment a run through," Keely said with a sigh. "Assuming I could find anything in the mess they left. Bradley kept some clothes at my place. Maybe it's there somewhere."

"Couldn't hurt to check." Lex pulled into a slot in front of Jeannie's shop.

"You don't need to park," Keely said quickly, but he was already turning off the key and getting out.

"I figured I'd come in, look around."

She frowned. "Somehow you don't strike me as a guy who's got a thing for flowers."

He gave her the same grin that had turned Lynette into putty. "I want to find something for my mom. She's had a tough time lately with all of this. I figure some flowers or a doodad might cheer her up."

"A doodad?"

"Technical term." He pulled open the door to Jeannie's. "After you, please."

Perfect. What she needed more than anything was time and space to think, to figure out what the heck was going on with her. Bad enough she'd promised to work the evening shift. The last thing she needed was Lex Alexander wandering around the shop, scrambling her emotions.

But only a complete Grinch would begrudge a guy who wanted to buy his mother a present.

"Hi, Keely." Lydia waved from where she was helping a customer behind the counter.

Keely waved back and turned her attention again

to Lex. The quicker she took care of him, the quicker she could send him on his way. That was what she wanted, wasn't it?

"So what are you looking for, flowers or a gift? We have some nice calla lilies. I think it's Olivia's favorite flower."

It was like a déjà vu, except that it wasn't Bradley coming in, begging her to choose a flower arrangement to make up for missing his mother's birthday, and it wasn't six years before. It was Lex and it was now. It was Lex and she hadn't a clue what she was feeling for him.

"I'm not sure what I'm looking for," he said easily. "Something she'll like." His hair flowed thick and dark down to his collar. Keely knew how soft it was.

She remembered the feel of it beneath her fingers.

She shook her head to banish the thought. The gift shop part of the store was where Jeannie indulged her love of design and whimsy. Handmade stationery and sculptured candles stood by Japanese porcelain sake carafes and French incense. Tapas cookbooks and lavender soap sat on embroidered Irish linen handkerchiefs. "What about that?"

"Soap?" He looked at her. "This is Olivia we're talking about."

"Okay, so no soap."

"Let's skip these glass doodads, too," he said, passing the snowflake-cut sun catchers.

Keely's lips twitched. "I thought you wanted a doodad."

"I do want a doodad, just not those doodads."

"Picky," she said.

He flicked a glance at her. "Generally. Now, this…" He stopped to look at a tiny sculpture of pale pink glass blossoms set on copper wires in a crystal vase, touching one with a fingertip.

"Nice choice," Keely said, biting back a sigh. "It's by one of our local artists. If you get it in the right light, the petals look almost real." It was also her favorite, but she'd resisted the urge to buy it. She needed to hold on to every penny just then in case she needed to pay for a lawyer.

The jingling of the door heralded the arrival of several customers at once, who pressed both Lydia and her into service. The next few minutes were a flurry of activity. Finally, though, the last bag was packed and the group was headed out the door.

Keely bent to get a new roll of cash register tape.

"Whoops, I've got to go get those vases ready for tomorrow," Lydia blurted. "I'll be in the back if you need me."

Keely rose just in time to see her bolting for the back.

And to see Lex approaching the counter.

She took a long, slow breath. "Find everything you were looking for?" she asked brightly.

"Just about." He set the little flower sculpture on the counter, as well as a cut crystal Baccarat vase that was sophisticated and traditional, just Olivia's taste.

"I see your definition of doodads ends on the large side," she said, wrapping the vase in layers of tissue paper and putting it into a carrier bag. She glanced at the glass flowers and ignored a twinge of regret. "We've got a box for that one in the back. Give me just a minute." She started to turn.

"Not necessary."

"It's too fragile to carry out," she objected. "It'll get broken."

"It's not going anywhere," he said. "It's for you."

It stopped her entirely. For a moment, she could only stare. "For me?"

Lex set it in front of her. "For you. My mom's not the only one having a tough time. I figured maybe you could use a doodad, too." He leaned over and pressed a kiss on her forehead. "Be well, Keely," he said, and walked out.

Chapter Seven

There were a variety of forms of hell on Earth. Living in a house while it was being renovated, for example. Chaperoning an overnight school trip of eleven-year-olds.

And being in a shopping mall a week and a half before Christmas.

"Who decided this was a good idea?" Keely demanded as they threaded their way through a department store.

Lydia stepped nimbly around a woman pushing two strollers. "You did. I believe you said something about having done zero Christmas shopping and needing to buy for everyone or you were going to be excommunicated from your family. True or false?"

"True," Keely sighed.

"Where do you want to start?"

"By making a run for the exits?"

"Not a chance. It took us forty-five minutes just to drive here. Now, who are you buying for?"

Keely jumped and shook her head hastily as a white coated sales clerk offered her a spritz of cologne. "Let's start with your shopping, first."

"Already done," Lydia said happily. "Target had a sale on Hello Kitty so I've got Melly's presents for the next ten years. Roy is happy with anything that has Nintendo on the label and the electronics store was offering two for one. I figure a quick pass through the lingerie store will take care of everyone else on my list."

"Everyone else you know needs lingerie?" Keely asked.

"Don't we all? Now, who are you buying for?"

Keely pondered. One thing she could say for the Bradley fiasco, her shopping list had abruptly gotten shorter. No work colleagues, no fiancé, no New York friends who'd proven not to be friends at all.

She looked at Lydia, loyal down to her last breath, the sister Keely had never had. They'd known each other since Jeannie's store first opened nearly eight years before. In the initial quiet days before the clientele had become steady, the two of them had had plenty of time to talk about everything under the sun. And talk, they had. It was a bond that never weakened, even when Keely moved away. No matter how busy she was whenever she visited Chilton, she always squeezed in lunch or coffee with Lydia.

"I need something for my Mom and Dad, of course," Keely said now, threading her way around a display of pre-wrapped moisturizer. "Darlene. And then I should shop for something that has absolutely nothing to do with you."

Lydia grinned and pointed to the jewelry department. "In that case, you should look over there by the purple sign. They've got a whole rack of absolutely nothing I would ever want to wear with my green satin dress when Roy and I go out for New Year's." She winked.

"I'll keep that in mind."

"Of course, it probably has absolutely nothing you'd want to wear if you wind up doing New Year's with Hunkzilla."

Keely frowned. "Hunkzilla?"

"You know, the hot guy who's been hanging around and giving you goodies?" Lydia prompted.

"Oh. Lex."

"Exactly. Bradley's brother, right? Looks like a much better substitution to me."

"Don't get any ideas. We're just trying to find a way out of this whole legal mess Bradley left."

"Two for one," Lydia nodded. "I can dig it."

"Lydia." Keely glowered at her.

"What? You can't tell me there's not any chemistry there."

"I'm not telling you anything," Keely replied. "I'm here to shop, not talk."

"You know," Lydia interrupted as they exited the department store into the mall, "I'm kinda hungry now that I think about it. Maybe we should start at the food court."

* * *

What was going on with her? Keely wondered as she sat on a hard red plastic chair and picked salt off her pretzel. Why was her brain so scrambled when it came to Lex?

"Look, I don't know why you're bugging me about him," she told Lydia. "After what went on with Bradley, I'd be out of my mind to get involved with any guy. Let alone another Alexander."

"They say after you fall off a horse you have to get right back on." Lydia forked up a bite of bourbon chicken.

"I don't even like him," Keely protested. Except that she knew it was a lie the minute she said it. The more she was around Lex, the more she got to know who he really was, the more she realized she like him quite a lot.

And then there were the butterflies.

"This is stupid." She scowled down at her Diet Coke. "It doesn't make any sense. I know it doesn't make any sense. But he touches me and I got nuts. And I shouldn't. I shouldn't want any part of this. So why do I?"

"He's your rebound guy," Lydia said matter-of-factly. "Your transitional man. Bradley sucked in the sack, big brother knows how it's done."

"We haven't been in the sack."

"Kissed you, whatever. The point is, Lex rows your boat."

"I don't need anyone to row my boat," Keely muttered.

"Sure you do, everyone does."

Keely's brows lowered. "Don't you need dessert? Maybe you should go get a Cinnabon or something."

Lydia shook her head. "Got to watch my weight to fit into that New Year's dress. And you are not getting out of this conversation, missy. Bradley hurt you and he messed your life around. Whether you were done with him by then or not, he still got to you, you can't deny it. And you can tell yourself all you like that you don't want anything to do with men, but this Lex isn't just any guy. He's what you need. Your body knows it even if your head doesn't."

Keely sulked. "You don't even know him."

"I've seen him with you. And Darlene likes him, which is good enough for me. You ever seen her be wrong about anyone?"

Keely opened her mouth and stopped.

"I didn't think so," Lydia said in satisfaction. "I'm just saying stop thinking about this so much. So what if he's not the perfect one for you? The guy works in Africa and the North Pole, for God's sake."

"The Middle East."

"Uh, yeah, well, you can't get much more transitional than that. The point is that he makes you feel good. I saw your face last night after he gave you the little vase. And I saw your face after the tree lighting, and don't say you didn't kiss him because I know you did. Stop over-thinking the situation. Just go with it." She rose. "Do *you* want a Cinnabon?"

The problem with being in Chilton, Lex thought as he walked around the town common with his camera, was that there was nothing for him to do outside of detecting. Oh, sure, he could check e-mail, he could make a few phone calls, but that burned maybe half an hour out of the day.

Leaving him way too much time to stare into space and think about Keely.

Less than a day had passed since they'd kissed in the woods. And there wasn't a moment of that time that he hadn't wanted her. It was like a constant hammering in his system, like some essence of her had slipped into him so that she had become a part of his every thought. It didn't matter about the country club, it didn't matter than she'd been engaged to Bradley. Everything Lex thought he'd known about her was wrong. She was on the level. And there was someone very different inside her, someone he'd never guessed existed.

In any other situation, with any other woman, he'd just keep after her until he changed her mind, he thought, pausing to take a couple of shots of the square brick bell tower that rose over Town Hall. And judging by the way she'd responded to that kiss, it wouldn't have taken much.

As kisses went, it was pretty damned hard to forget. He did his best not to think about it, to convince his body that it wasn't happening, at least not now. Because the part after the kiss was also indelibly stamped in his memory—the look on her face, the shadows and confusion in her eyes when she'd pleaded with him. *I'm still trying to get over one Alexander. I don't need to go onto another.*

What the hell was a guy supposed to do with something like that? What he'd done, Lex supposed. With an absent frown, he emptied the coins out of his pocket into the Salvation Army bell ringer's bucket and walked on toward the common. So now he was stuck waiting around, hoping that Keely would get past whatever his idiot brother had done to her.

And hoping to God it happened before he got sent back out into the wild blue yonder and they lost their chance forever.

Out of the corner of his eye, he caught a flick of motion as something arced low across the sky. Adrenaline surged. Before he could think, muscle memory had him ducking behind a bench. An instant later, he rose, shaking his head at himself. And he saw it again—a sphere of white against the blue sky. Snowball fight, he thought. Just a holiday snowball fight.

And what did it say about his life that his first thought had been that it was incoming?

He could see them now, a collection of boys maybe ten or eleven, a couple of them socked in behind the Revolutionary War cannon, methodically going through their stocked-up ammo while the opposition fired from behind the fountain. The cannon was the best location, Lex remembered from when he was a kid—better sight lines, higher ground. He and Bradley had defended it more than once, even when they'd been significantly outnumbered.

Grinning, Lex circled the common, snapping shots rhythmically, capturing the narrow-eyed focus, the strategy, the glee of a direct shot. Christmas vacation in Chilton. Some things never changed.

He was still grinning an hour later when he walked into the house to see Olivia.

"What have you been up to?" she asked.

"Knocking around, taking some shots."

"Cub photographer, on the job." Her smile faded. "I still have the camera Nana bought you. You didn't take it when you left."

"No choice. I couldn't take everything." But it had changed his life. From the time he'd gotten the camera at twelve, photography had been all he'd cared about. It had driven Pierce wild. He hadn't wanted to know about art classes or the awards Lex won, just moved Lex to a school that didn't deal in that sort of thing. Olivia tried to support him from behind the scenes but there was little she could do when Pierce got an idea in his head.

"I'm glad you're back. I need your help," she said now, glancing down at the papers in her hands. "Some bills and things have come over the past few days. I'm not sure what to do with them. I always set them aside for Bradley." She looked up, a hint of pink staining her cheeks. "Can you help?"

Lex raised his brows. "Are you sure you're ready to trust another one of your sons with your money?"

"You're not Bradley," she responded tartly and handed him the stack. "I just need to learn how it works."

"Mom, you're talking to a guy who lives in the field," Lex protested, flipping through the swath of bills and statements. "I don't have things like utilities. Every bill I do have is hooked up to my checking account to get paid automatically."

"Perhaps that's what I need to do. Can you help?"

He bit back a sigh. "Yeah, let's go look it over."

He walked into the office with familiar sense that he was stepping back into a world where Pierce still might come walking in at any moment. Even the same art hung on the walls, down to the photo of Pierce and some of his cronies with the president.

He saw Olivia glance at it and blink.

"Why don't you redecorate in here?" he suggested. "It might make it easier on you."

"It would seem like wiping him out of my life," she said in a low voice. "I changed the rest of the house but this part, this is still him."

"Is that a blessing or a curse?"

"I'm not sure," she said.

Lex studied her. "Why did you marry him?" He asked it before he knew he was going to.

Olivia stilled.

"Forget it." He shook his head and sat at the desk. "You don't have to answer that."

Olivia didn't take the out, though. Instead, she took her time settling on the upholstered chair that sat before the desk, crossing her legs, studying her hands.

"Things don't always turn out like you expect," she said finally. "In the beginning, I thought he was just confident. It was exciting to be with a man who made the world do his bidding. It was only later that I realized that it applied to us, too. When you're young, you don't realize that people only become more so as they get older." She toyed with her rings.

"And maybe I changed, too. I was so young when we married and just starry-eyed over him. He was good-looking, so obviously going places. And he wanted me. Me," she repeated, still sounding amazed.

"It shouldn't surprise you."

"It does. I felt like I was living a dream, like he was my prince. When I grew up enough that I wanted him to share the running of our lives and our family, he thought that I was suddenly changing the rules on him. It made him angry. As far as he was concerned, he was doing the same thing he always had. And maybe he was, except instead of giving orders to his staff, he was giving them to his family."

"You tried to protect us."

Her laugh was short and bitter. "I didn't do very well, did I? Not if you had to run away."

"I was eighteen. It was time."

"To go off to college, maybe. Not to disappear."

"I'd had all I could take." He remembered that last afternoon, the hard words, the lightness he'd felt as he stood on the shoulder of the highway watching a truck slow down to pick him up.

"I'd have left him if he'd ever raised a hand to any of us. He never did."

Lex gave a faint smile. "Like those frogs they put in water that heats up so slowly they don't realize they're on their way to being boiled alive."

"Not that bad, I don't think. Or maybe it was. I'd like to think he was better after you left, but maybe I just didn't care." She let out a sigh. "In the end, we came to an accommodation. I miss him. Hard to understand, I know, but I do. For better or worse, that's what the vows say."

"Was it ever for better?"

To his surprise, she nodded. "There were some good times. You don't remember them—maybe you don't want to—but they were there." She paused. "Bill Hartley is calling me again."

"Interesting segue."

"You shouldn't avoid it just because you're still angry at your father. This is bigger than that."

"I already told you, I'm not interested." Restlessly, Lex toyed with the gold pen on the desk set.

Olivia watched him. "It would come with a block of stock."

"I don't need a block of stock."

"Of course you do. The price is down because of this situation with Bradley but it'll come back up, especially with your leadership."

He shook his head and reached out to the glass bowl to pick out a pair of steel balls that sat atop the paper-clips. Bogie in *The Caine Mutiny,* rolling the balls in his hand. "I don't have any leadership to offer. I don't know anything about the business."

"You could. You should," she added.

"I'm a photographer, not a business exec. I'm not cut out for a desk." The steel balls clicked. "Alexander Technologies will survive without me. Pierce was right about one thing—" He broke off at the burble of his cell phone. "I'd better get this."

"A phone call, someone at the door… Trey, you can't keep evading this conversation. We need to finish it," Olivia said.

"As far as I'm concerned, we already have," Lex returned.

She didn't answer, just turned and walked out of the room, closing the door behind her.

Lex glanced at the phone display to see the number of his New York boss, Joe Flaherty. "Joe, my man, you've never had better timing than now," he murmured, flipping the phone open and leaning back in his chair. "Yeah."

"Lex?"

"Joe. What's up?"

"Glad I caught you. How's things at home?"

Lex rolled the steel balls in his hand. "All right, as long as you don't ask me for up close and personal wire photos of the Alexander Technologies scandal." *Click. Click.*

"Rough time?" Joe asked sympathetically.

"Makes the Kalahari look like a tea party."

"Who knew suburban Connecticut was such a struggle? Feel like taking a break?"

"Not if you're planning to send me out of this time zone. Things are sticky enough around here."

"Ah, laddie, d'ya think I'd do that while you're in town to take care of your sainted mother?" Flaherty's words held a sudden breath of County Clare.

Lex snorted. "For the right shot, Flaherty, I think you'd sell your grandma."

"Quite possibly true." Flaherty's voice reverted to its normal nasal Philly accent. "But in this case, I just thought you might want to come into the city."

"Come into the city?"

"Lunch, on me."

Lex sat up, eyes narrowed. "What have you got up your sleeve, Flaherty?"

"What makes you think I've got anything up my sleeve?" Flaherty asked with pretended affront.

"Ever heard the phrase 'there's no such thing as a free lunch'?"

"You hurt me, young Aubrey."

"You're never going to let me forget that, are you?" Lex sighed. His professional byline was Lex Alexander. It had been a long, late night of drinking more than a decade before when he'd broken down and confessed his real name to Joe.

"Would you deny an old man his little pleasures?"

"You're not an old man, Flaherty."

"I still like my little pleasures."

"There's something just a little perverse about the sound of that," Lex said, moving to toss the balls back into the bowl. They landed with a little *chunk* atop paperclips and detritus of business life accumulating in his father's glass bowl. *I think Bradley just started tossing things in there.*

The hair on the back of his neck prickled.

"Are you going to come in or not, Alexander?" Flaherty demanded.

What were the chances it hadn't been searched? Then again, why would they care about a key? How many unidentifiable old keys were floating around the average house? Pulling the bowl toward him, he began rummaging through the contents. Paperclips, rubber bands, binder clips, a couple of Phillips head screws, an adaptor for a headphone jack, more paperclips.

And jammed in the middle of it all, a key.

There was a noise in his ear and Lex shook his head. "Sorry, Joe, what did you say?"

"I said are you there?"

"I'm here." He tipped the mess out onto the desktop, untangling the key from it all. A house key, he thought, turning it over in his palm.

"The question is, are you going to be here?" Flaherty asked. "Say, day after tomorrow?"

"Sure," Lex said. "Listen, Joe, I gotta go. E-mail me the time and place and I'll be there." He hung up and stared at the key in his hand.

Chapter Eight

"One coffee, two lattes, one skim, no crullers," Keely ordered.

"One coffee, two lattes, one skim," Darlene repeated. "And no crullers."

"No crullers." Keely's voice was wistful.

Darlene put the coffee order together with brisk efficiency. "One coffee, two lattes, one skim," she said, handing Keely a cardboard carrier full of steaming cups. "And no crullers."

"No very tasty-looking crullers," Keely agreed.

"Ixnay on the crullers."

"Exactly. Have a good afternoon." Keely turned away and took one step, then another. Then stopped and whirled around. "Crullers," she demanded, "three of them."

"Crullers, it is," Darlene said, fighting a smile as she snapped open the waxed paper pastry bag she was holding. "You know, you almost made it out the door this time. I was rooting for you, kid."

"It's the smell," Keely told her in exasperation. "If you didn't make the best coffee in town, I could go somewhere else, but you do and then I have to walk in here and smell everything you've baked and I'm just toast."

"So to speak."

"So to speak."

"How's the hunt for clues going?"

"Not fast enough. If we don't find something soon, I'm going to be as big as a house."

Darlene eyed Keely's willowy frame as she folded the top on the bag of pastries. "That, I doubt. Anyway, consider your buying habits a personal favor to me. If you eat the crullers, then I have to go make more, which gives me constructive work to do, which means I have at least two or three hours to avoid doing my end-of-quarter tax forms."

"Your 941?" Keely asked.

Darlene made a cross with her forefingers. "Back, demon. Don't speak those words here."

"Darlene, a culinary genius like yourself should not be wasting her time doing tax paperwork. Don't you have an accountant?"

"I did but he moved a couple of months back. I just haven't had time to find anyone else." Her lips twitched. "Too busy making crullers."

"Well, you should have told me sooner. I spent a whole internship at Briarson just doing tax work and payroll." Keely slid a bill across the counter and took the bag of crullers. "Listen, I've got to get back to the store but I've got some time tomorrow morning. Let me come by and take a look. I'm sure I can get you fixed up." Keely stopped. "Of course, you may not want a 'person of interest' in a money-laundering case working on your books."

"The heck with that. It's Bradley they're after, not you. It's just that you're supposed to be here lying low, not working."

"It's okay."

"But—"

"No buts. Just say yes and thank you and be done with it."

"Bossy," Darlene said, handing her change.

Keely grinned. "So I've been told."

The air outside was brisk, the sky a crystalline blue. Keely headed back toward Jeannie's, stopping only to dump her change in the Salvation Army bucket.

"Thank you, young lady," said the bell ringer.

"Anytime, Harvey." She flashed him a smile and walked on.

It was funny. She hadn't wanted to come back to Chilton. She'd dreaded it, expected it to be stifling, boring, tiresome. Instead, it was cozy. She slept without waking to sirens, got to work in the morning without the crush of the subway. There was something about her daily schtick with Darlene, something about the sense of community that had always been missing in New York.

Not that she wanted to stay or anything, of course.

She enjoyed having a career, even if, truth be told,

the corporate world had proven to be both more stressful and less interesting than she'd imagined it would be. Which raised the all too scary question of what to do about Briarson. Even if they welcomed her back with open arms after she cleared her name, the fact of the matter was still that the company hadn't stood behind her. They hadn't cared about the long hours, the hard work she'd put in over the years. They hadn't believed in her.

When push came to shove, they'd looked after themselves.

As she needed to do. Of course, there was the little matter of paying for rent and food, so she'd have to get busy sending out resumes pretty soon.

"There you are."

At the impatient words, Keely glanced up to see Lex striding toward her and her stomach did a little somersault. "Hey."

"Where have you been? I tried calling your cell."

"It's at the shop." She found herself oddly breathless. "I went to get coffee." She raised the carrier.

He took the carrier from her. "So your mother said."

"Tell me you didn't talk to Lydia," Keely groaned.

"The redhead? Why?"

"Never mind. What's going on?"

Lex waved something before her.

"What's that?"

"What does it look like?" he asked.

"A key," she said absently, and then did a double-take. *"A key?"*

"Yep. I found it on the desk in Pierce's office. The one Bradley used."

"The key to the house," she breathed.

"There's no guarantee but I think there's a better than average chance. Smart, if you think about it. He's got a safe house that doesn't show up on any of his books or the books of his LLCs. The key's not on him, in his condo, or hidden around the house where someone might find it. All he has to do is stop by my mom's, say hi, and scoot over there sometime while he's in town."

Her heart began to hammer against her ribs. "Have you tried it?"

He raised a brow. "I was waiting for you, partner. Can you drop off the coffee and get away from here for an hour or two?"

"Definitely." She grinned. "Partner."

The house was easier to find the second time around. In full daylight, with the early afternoon sun shining, the forlorn air was gone. It looked bright and clean and almost charming.

"I bet it's really gorgeous out here in summer." Keely studied the woods that sloped away from them.

"Probably so. I doubt Bradley bought the place for the view, though." They stood on the side porch by the door. Curtains inside kept them from seeing into the room beyond. Lex raised the key to the lock. "Okay, cross your fingers."

"Fingers crossed, sir," she reported.

He pushed and the key slid smoothly into place. "Good sign," he commented.

Keely's heart began to thud against her ribs. "Toes crossed, also, sir."

Lex flashed her a grin and moved to turn the key. It rotated smoothly in the lock with a little snick, and then the doorknob was turning, as well.

And the door opened sweetly before them.

They walked into a small mud room, which opened out into a daisy yellow kitchen. Their rubber-soled shoes were quiet on the linoleum as they walked past the white tile counters. Under other circumstances, it was probably a cheerful room, with its sunny walls and windowed breakfast nook. Shuttered and silent, though, it only gave her a profound sense of trespassing. It didn't matter why they were there, it still felt wrong.

Lex opened the refrigerator to find it empty and turned off.

"Let's hurry," she whispered.

One end of the kitchen looked out to the entryway and the great room. Big, was Keely's first thought. Bigger than it had appeared from the outside. Also open, also empty, as in devoid of furniture.

"Guess he believes in the minimalist thing," Keely said in a hushed voice, looking around.

"Minimalist as in nothing." Lex pushed open the door to the half bath to find it empty of even towels or paper.

Keely peeked in. "I suppose that means it's a home for data, not people."

"Good guess."

The place was surprisingly bright despite the drapes on the windows, courtesy of a trio of skylights that brought sunlight in from above. Keely and Lex wandered through the big open living room, stepping up onto carpet that was thick and plush. Had the drapes been open, the wall of windows would have brought the woods inside. Had the drapes been open, it would have been lovely.

"Poor house," Keely said. "Someone probably loved it once and now it just sits up here, empty and alone."

Lex flipped a switch and a light came on. "Not entirely empty if someone's got the power on." He flipped it back off. "I guess something's working somewhere."

"He's got to have juice. Unless everything's hard copy, he's got to have a computer."

Lex nodded. "So let's find it."

They headed down the hallway that led to the bedrooms.

"So much for wood stoves." Keely pointed to a thermostat on the wall and stopped to turn it up. There was a tiny flash of light and a brief hum and they heard the sound of a furnace kicking in somewhere.

She shook her head as they continued down the hall to find the first bedroom empty. "Heat and power, but no furniture. It makes no sense."

The second room was empty also, sunlight showing below the curtains covering the windows.

And the third?

"Jackpot," Lex said softly.

The room held a wide, plush black leather couch. Before it sat a coffee table with the usual jumble of remotes and coasters and magazines. On the opposite wall hung a flat-screen television. To one side sat a sleek gray desk.

"It's got to be somewhere in this room." Lex bent to the desk.

As though they'd been assigned jobs, Keely turned

to the closet. It was bare, at a glance. She opened up the built-in wall cabinets alongside. The top one was empty. The wide drawer below protested as she pulled it out, its runners binding before it relented to let her find it empty, too. The drawer below that was in similarly bad shape. The bottom drawer, however, slid out smoothly. And it was there that she found it—the black mesh fabric of a laptop case.

"Oh, come to Mama," Keely breathed.

Lex turned to see her pulling out the case. "Sweet."

"It will be once we find what we want." Nerves made her hands shake a little as she brought the laptop out and set it on the desk.

Lex continued looking through the drawers.

"Anything?" Keely asked.

He shook his head. "I'm betting it's all going to be electronic. Easy to store, easy to transport. Easy to forward to his colleague if he needs to offer a reminder."

Keely gave a little shiver as she thought of Skele. "I would think he'd want to avoid him as much as possible."

"Why? From Bradley's point of view, the guy is his meal ticket. That's where the money comes from, and I'm betting that he has as much on Skele as Skele has on him."

Except Bradley didn't kill people for a living.

The laptop hummed and finished booting up, flashing the login screen. The username was there, the password line empty. "I was afraid of that," Keely said, hitting the enter key. *Password not recognized. Please reenter.*

"We should have expected it. Most computers come up with a login screen," Lex pointed out.

"It's still a problem." She typed in Bradley's name. *Password not recognized. Please reenter.*

"You tried his first name?"

"Just did," she said, making a frustrated noise as the computer obstinately displayed the same message. "And his last name. And your parents'. Let's think about this. People usually pick names of things or people that are important to them. What would that be?"

"Yours?" Lex suggested.

She snorted but tried it anyway. "No dice."

"I suppose you tried just hitting Enter to bypass?"

She didn't bother to answer, just flicked him a glance from under her brows and began looking around on the desktop, on the bottom of the computer, in the drawers.

"What are you looking for?"

"The password." She slid out the breadboard, examined it, and pushed it back in. "Bradley can never remember his passwords. He always writes them down somewhere."

"It's probably in his wallet," Lex said, joining the search.

"He doesn't carry a wallet. Too bulky. He has this little glorified money clip thing that also keeps a couple of credit cards and his license. No, if he's true to form, it'll be here."

Except that it wasn't.

"Maybe it's somewhere else in the house," Lex suggested.

"Can't hurt to check, I suppose." Reluctantly, she rose.

They headed out into the dimness of the hall, inspecting closets, cabinets and even the bathroom they passed, only to find them all empty. Ahead was the master bedroom. They stepped through the door and stopped dead.

"More of that minimalist thing," Lex observed.

It was filled with a single piece of furniture—an enormous four-poster bed. No mirror, no bed table, no bureau, no chair. No lamps. Just a smooth, square slab nearly the size of Rhode Island, covered with a deep wine-colored duvet and a pair of pillows.

Keely stared in silence. "Why would he need a bed?" she asked finally.

"To sleep in?"

"If he wanted to sleep, he has the couch." Not this enormous, frankly opulent bed. She couldn't say what prompted her, but she crossed suddenly to the wall cabinets and opened the door.

To find a small, tidy stack of sheets.

She sank down on the soft mattress, feeling it give under her. "It's an empty house. No furniture, no dishes, no towels. No light bulbs in most of the fixtures. Even the refrigerator's empty. He didn't stay here." Her voice tightened. "Why would he need a bed?" She glanced down.

And then she saw it.

A long, dark hair curled across the pillow.

Unbidden, her imagination conjured up an image of Bradley there, naked, with a woman wrapped around him, the two of them hot and sweaty and crying out as he cheated on her, cheated on her, cheated on her....

Cheated on her.

She turned to Lex. "Have sex with me."

He stared. "What?"

She slid her jacket off her shoulders. "Have sex with me. Now." She dropped the jacket on the floor and crossed to shut the door, shivering a bit despite herself at the chill in the air.

"Whoa. Wait a second. What's going on?"

"I think it's a pretty simple request. You wanted it the other night, unless you've changed your mind. And Bradley's very considerately put this nice, big bed here." Her hands dropped to the buttons of her shirt. "I say we use it." She freed the bottom button.

"You're nuts."

"You don't want me?" she demanded, a hard, bright, merciless light in her eyes.

"This doesn't have anything to do with me. As near as I can tell, this is about you and Bradley."

She unfastened another button and walked up to him, her movements feline. "Come on." She leaned in to breathe the words over his lips. "It'll be good. You know it."

Against his will, he felt himself tightening, but anger swamped the desire. "I'm not a tool here, lady. I'm already cleaning up one of Bradley's messes. I don't want to clean up another."

She whirled away, two spots of color burning high on her cheeks. "I'm a mess? Thanks very much for that."

Now he was the one who stalked up to her. "Don't put words in my mouth. You want to go to bed and it's about you and me, done, I'm there in a heartbeat. But I am not going to be your revenge lay."

"Who asked you to be? You don't know what I'm thinking."

"Why did you and Bradley break up?" he asked evenly.

She whitened. "That's none of your business."

"The hell it's not. Why did you and Bradley break up?"

"I'm not going to tell you." She tried to step away but he caught at her shoulders.

"Why did you and Bradley break up?"

"Let me go!"

"Why did you and Bradley break up?"

"Because he was an evil, lying sonofabitch," she burst out.

The words echoed in the air for long moments. Keely could hear each separate beat of her heart. Her gaze was locked on Lex's, she couldn't look away.

"What did he do to you?" His voice was soft.

"He was cheating on me." She kept her voice dry, scrubbed of emotion. "I stopped by his house during the day to get some things and I walked in on him doing Kama Sutra pose number 28B with some woman, complete with Dolby stereo sound effects."

"Jesus."

"It was a surprise," she agreed. "And then I went back to my house, just to get my head together and found Stockton and his buddies tossing the place and telling me my name was connected with money laundering and fraud."

"Jesus."

"In a word." Her smile held no humor. "I've had better mornings. Oh, and then two days later, my boss told me to disappear for a while because of the newspaper headlines. And then I come here to find a bed that he's obviously used with someone..." She swallowed. "So yeah, revenge sounds pretty damned good right now. Are you in?"

He leaned in and pressed his lips to her forehead. "No. Not that way. I don't want to sleep with you because you're trying to get back at the guy you're in love with because he hurt you."

"I'm not in love with Bradley. I haven't been for a while, even before that day." She walked over to stare out of the narrow opening in the bedroom drapes. Leafless trees, stark and barren and colorless. "I was going to break up with him that night. That's why I went to his apartment, to get my stuff."

"Why? Had you found out?"

She shook her head. "Not directly, not about any of it. I just...it started feeling wrong a little while after we got engaged. Like we were just going through the motions. He was my Prince Charming from when I was a girl but we were grownups now and we weren't living in Far Far Away. It just felt like we'd be sorry. Like I would be," she amended. "So I went over to get my stuff so I could tell him that night."

"And you found him."

She tried for a smile that didn't make it. "Funny thing about being humiliated. Even when you're not in love with the guy, it still feels like hell." And to her utter mortification, she felt tears prick her eyelids.

"He was an idiot," Lex said softly. He moved to her and slid his arms around her waist. "He was out of his mind to cheat on you." He leaned down to drop a kiss on her hair, on her forehead, on her eyes.

It started out as comfort, nothing more. She opened

her eyes to stare up into his and find the anger gone, replaced by kindness. When they touched their mouths together, it was with the innocence of the very young. It was connection, reassurance.

And then it changed.

Keely didn't know who changed the angle of the kiss, whose lips parted first. Like a twist of the thermostat firing the furnace, the friction of lip to lip sparked an answering response in her body, a desire poised to grow into need. Lex's arms tightened around her. The heat between them rose and suddenly the kiss wasn't about comfort anymore.

For days they'd circled around it, like moths around a candle. Now, they weren't circling. Now, there wasn't any reason to stop. Now, they were here in this private place, just the two of them, and the stalling was done.

Now, they were both diving for the flame.

His fingers slid between them, unfastening the remaining buttons on her shirt even as she pushed his jacket off his shoulders and let it drop to the floor. Then he stepped in to pull her against him, to take her mouth, possess it, plunder it.

And it was marvelous.

Keely let her head fall back and in a giddy delight she felt Lex's tongue trace a warm path down to the base of her neck. He pressed his lips against the hollow in her throat as if he were drawing sustenance from her, as though his life depended on it. And his hands, his hands were doing wonderful things, roving up and down her body, sliding and caressing so that even through the clothing she wore, her nerve endings awoke.

Sex with Bradley had always been measured and quiet. She'd been aroused but within limits. She didn't want limits anymore. She wanted, needed to be ravished. She wanted to be taken.

She wanted to lose control.

"It wasn't like this," she said unsteadily. "Not like it is between you and me, it was never like that with Bradley."

"We haven't even started yet," Lex said against her skin.

Oh, but they were going to. This time, there wouldn't be any interruptions. This time, they would do it all. Clothing was an impediment, to be thrown aside as quickly as possible. And then they were naked, on the bed, and she'd never felt anything so glorious.

His body was lean, tough. He didn't have the smooth, exaggerated physique of a gym junkie but the hard-muscled build of a man who spent his days in motion, lifting, carrying, working.

He curved his hand around her cheek and drew it slowly down over her jaw, along her throat. The first time they'd seen each other again, she'd wondered what his hands would feel like running over her. Her imagination hadn't even come close. And every touch just made her burn to have his touch on the pulsing places where she craved him most.

He traced his fingertips down to where the tender, fragile skin of her breast began and Keely gasped. "Please," she whispered.

"No," he said. Instead, he just kept tracing his fingers around first one breast, then the other. When she made an impatient noise, he ignored her, taking his time, tormenting her with pleasure, spiraling in toward the center, leaning in to watch in fascination as the ruddy flesh of her areolas crinkled up around the hard nubs of her nipples.

How was it that such a whisper-light touch could send need rocketing through her? How could his circling fingertips feel like they were setting her afire? And how was it possible that she could feel the sensation radiating out from her nipples when his circling fingers were still on the pale skin of her breasts?

Lex leaned in and blew a stream of air over the sensitive flesh and she gasped. Eyes closed, she heard his low laugh. And with a suddenness that had her body bucking in shock, he fastened his mouth over her.

Warm and wet, quick and teasing, his lips and tongue had her crying out, pressing against him. He took his time, focusing on first one peak, then the other until she was moaning feverishly, tangling her fingers in his hair. When she didn't think she could bear any more, he lingered longer.

And then he moved lower, his tongue tracing patterns on the quivering skin of her belly.

Keely was trembling, she knew she was trembling as he roved over her body, pleasing himself, stringing her as tight as a wire. She waited, breathless. The ache between her thighs grew.

The brush of his cheek against the soft skin of her inner thigh had her jolting. Warm breath flowed over her most sensitive places and still, still, he didn't touch her where she burned for it. Her fingers clutched the sheets as she struggled not to beg.

Then his mouth was on her, hot and wet and relentless.

It was too much to bear, too intense, too direct. Her entire world reduced down to that liquid caress. She didn't recognize the sound that came from her throat, something urgent and completely wild. His hands were on her breasts. She was melting under the warmth, her hips moving as the sensation built in the center of her. Every atom of her body was focused on that exquisitely sensitive spot where his mouth, that delicious, clever, talented mouth was winding her tighter and tighter until it was unbearable, until she was crying out incoherently, thrashing her head from side to side on the pillow, certain she couldn't take a millisecond more. And then she was flung over the edge, flying apart, endlessly flying apart into a million shimmering fragments of pleasure.

Even as she was still shuddering from her climax, he moved up the bed. They pressed together again, touching, stroking, enticing, until the need pulsed within her, the need to have him all the way.

"I want you," she whispered.

He moved atop her, lying between her thighs. "Are you sure?" he asked, his face taut with the need for control.

In answer, she reached out to pull his hips toward her. She could feel him positioning himself, the slide of his hard flesh against her slickness almost unbearably arousing.

"Please. Now." Her voice was ragged.

With a pump of his hips, he slid all the way home inside her, dragging a cry from them both. It was too intense to bear, Keely thought, the feel of him inside her, on her, against her, around her, his open mouth against her throat.

And then he raised his head to stare down into her eyes and he began to move. The first thrust had her gasping. She could feel him with every particle of her being. His fingers wove through her hair and he stroked into her, hard and fierce, his muscles bunching and flowing as he made her a part of him and himself a part of her. Never like this, she thought feverishly, it had never been like this before with Bradley, with anyone. She slid her fingers down his back, wrapped her legs around his waist.

"More," she demanded. "Don't stop."

He slid one hand under her hips, brought a leg up to curl around her and rolled over onto his back, taking her with him. "I've got a better idea, cowgirl," he said. "Why don't you ride?"

And then she was on top of him, straddling him, his hands on her hips helping her find the rhythm and she'd never felt a man go so deep. She moved against him instinctively, feeling an intensity of pleasure that was so exquisitely sharp it was impossible to say where it ended and pain began. Part of her wanted to slow down and savor but she couldn't because the need was too strong, the need for that rush of pleasure that flooded through her with every stroke, bringing her up and further up, building the tension that was impossible, unbearable, except that if she had to stop she'd die and every stroke she needed another to be sure that, yes, it was real, it was that good…and better…and better.

He was inside her and touching her, his hands now on her breasts, now below. Never like this, the words pounded through her, never like this, never like this, never like—

And she felt herself break and better became incredible. It flooded through her, sending her bucking against him, crying out mindlessly and, shockingly, it went on, rising to an even higher crest before slowly, softly ebbing away. And even as she still shook with it, she watched Lex's face tighten as though he was in pain and he groaned with his own release, pulling her down onto him, hard.

Lex lay, waiting for his pulse to stop thundering, waiting for the strength to return to his muscles. He wasn't sure how long it would take. He hadn't experienced anything quite like this before.

Keely stirred atop him. "Am I too heavy? Should I move?"

His hands tightened on her back. "No, you're fine." He wanted a few more minutes to just lie there, savoring the soft, slight weight of her draped over him like some human blanket, their bodies intimately linked.

She looked down at him, her eyes large and dark. He tucked her hair behind her ears. "You okay?"

"I'm not sure what I am." She propped her elbows on the pillow to either side of his head. "Stunned, maybe."

"It was quite something." He pressed a kiss to her mouth. "You're quite something." And he already wanted her again.

As though she'd heard his thought, she glanced at the darkening window. Outside, the day was stretching into late afternoon. "We probably ought to get going. I don't think we want to be driving down that road in the dark. Should we take the computer?"

"No. There's no telling when he might be back. We should leave here with everything just like it was when we got here."

Keely stood, glancing at the tumbled bed. "That might take some doing."

Which was saying a mouthful, Lex thought as they dressed. Having sex probably wasn't the smartest thing they could have done, but they were both adults and you could only ignore chemistry for so long. It had been worth it, probably the most amazing sex he'd ever had in his life.

A little flicker of uneasiness passed through him. He gave himself a quick mental shake. Special, yes. Memorable, yes. Not for the long term, though. They were both following different paths. If they could be together for the time he remained in Chilton, great. Good times, great memories, no ties. They'd find the data they needed, take care of the legal issues, go back to living their separate lives.

And why the hell did the thought depress him?

Chapter Nine

"You did what?" Lydia stopped and stared at Keely.

"I had sex with him."

The morning was crisp, the streets whitened by overnight snowfall. They were taking what had become their habitual early morning walk through Chilton. It was part of Lydia's campaign to fit into her New Year's dress, but it had become as much an excuse to talk as anything.

"You had sex with him," Lydia repeated, walking again. "I thought you'd decided not to do that."

"I thought I had, too. It just…happened."

"Oh, yeah. I know about that one." Lydia flicked her a speculative glance. "So?"

"What?"

"How was it? Is he an up-all-night kind of guy? You

have that up-all-night look. Actually," she reconsidered, "you look wiped."

"That's because I didn't sleep. Not because I was with Lex," she hastened to add. "We did our thing in the afternoon." Then she'd gone home and tossed and turned half the night, and when morning dawned, she'd had no better understanding of herself.

Lydia gave her a suspicious look. "Are you over-thinking things again?"

"I don't know," Keely said as they crossed to the town common. "I don't know what I'm doing. I don't know if this is just about Lex and me or if it's still some-thing to do with Bradley. I didn't think so yesterday, but what if it's some weird subconscious thing?"

"You *are* overthinking."

Keely bent down and picked up a pinecone that lay on the snow. "What I'm doing is things that don't make sense," she grumbled.

"You're allowed. Rebound sex happens all the time, especially after a bad breakup. And you've gotta admit, your experience with Bradley qualifies."

"Yeah, rebound sex, sure, but with a guy's *brother?*"

Lydia opened her mouth and closed it. "You've got your reasons."

"Or maybe I'm just more screwed up about the situation than I think."

"Or maybe it's real."

Keely was silent, listening to the crunch of their footsteps in the snow. Across the common, garland and glass balls glittered on the town Christmas tree. "It was like nothing I've ever felt before with anyone," she said finally. "There's something about the way he touches me… It feels real. But how do I know?"

"Stop dissecting it. Forget about Bradley, forget about this whole legal mess. If you and Lex just met at a club or the grocery store or at the QuickLube getting your oil changed—"

"The QuickLube?"

"Don't laugh, that's how my cousin and her husband met. Of course, they're getting divorced now. But still. The point is, if you guys just met as people, you wouldn't be putting it all under the microscope like this, would you?"

"How am I supposed to know?" Keely burst out. "You can't take away Bradley, you can't take away the whole mess. It's *there*. If none of that existed, Lex would be in Africa or the North Pole or wherever. And the minute this is over, he'll be back there. He'll be on a plane, I'll be in New York and that will be that." She flung the pinecone away. "I've got to be out of my mind," she muttered. "I can't get involved with this guy."

Lydia put a sympathetic arm around her shoulders. "Too late, girlfriend, I think you already are."

Lex pushed open the door to the flower shop and inhaled the now-familiar confusion of floral scents. Sure, he could have just called Keely's cell phone. He didn't need to go find her at the shop. So what? The plain and simple truth of it was that he wanted to see her. And if that meant tracking her down, then that was what he'd do.

Tracking, it appeared, would be required because

she was nowhere to be seen. "Is Keely around?" he asked the curvy redhead he'd seen behind the counter before.

She gave him an appraising look, opening her mouth as though she might say something, then closing it again. She nodded toward the open doorway behind her. "She's out back."

"Thanks." Lex walked past her into the rear work area. Up front, the shop looked like an Aladdin's cave, flowers intermingling with wind chimes and dishes and ornaments and books and a whole host of artsy knick-knacks that he couldn't identify. The back area was strictly functional, the treasures packed up in cardboard boxes, the flowers jammed into racks of utilitarian black buckets.

Which was a good thing, because spread over nearly every flat surface, and a few that weren't so flat, were what seemed like hundreds of low, wide, green glass vases with white bell-shaped flowers spilling out of them. They were grouped into pairs in shallow, black trays for carrying.

And the person doing the carrying, he saw, was Keely.

She was facing away from him, using one foot to drag open the back door while trying to balance the arrangements. He heard a woman's voice from the outside, saying something he couldn't quite catch over the radio playing. A joke, apparently, because Keely laughed, a rippling sound of pleasure.

Then she glanced over and saw him and her smile bloomed, quick and sure and lovely, and for a minute all he wanted in the world was to hold on to that image, that feeling, that moment in time.

She stumbled and bobbled the tray.

Lex scrambled across the room to grab it just as it started to really tip, and took it from her grasp. "Okay, I've got it," he said, and hefted it a bit in surprise. "Heavier than they look."

"It's the water," she explained. "Thanks for getting it. If I'd dropped them, Mom would have had my neck."

"Pity. It's a gorgeous neck."

Surprise, pleasure and a flick of uneasiness, he saw them all run through her eyes. Above the flowers, he caught that scent that was hers alone, something subtle and elusive and beckoning. He watched as her tongue crept out to moisten her lips. Before she could speak, though, the door opened up and Jeannie Stafford burst inside.

"The next time I agree to do flowers for Nancy Pittman, have my head examined," she ordered. "Lily of the valley in January? For fifty tables? The woman's out of her mind. Who invites three hundred people to her daughter's wedding? They can't possibly have that many friends, I should know. Come on, let's get these flowers out here or they're all going to get burned by the cold," she continued on, barely drawing breath as she kicked down the door stop. "Hello, Lex. Can you help us out since you're here? What are you doing here?"

"Conscript labor, apparently," Keely muttered as Lex picked up another tray of what he now guessed were centerpieces.

"Bless your heart." Jeannie hoisted one herself. "Good to see the Christmas spirit is alive and well in Chilton."

With surprising speed, given the weight of the arrangements, she marched out into the alley where a green-and-white cargo van waited, the interior fitted with racks for holding the trays. Already, a number of the slots were filled. Jeannie slid her tray into place then scrambled into the van to load Keely and Lex's trays.

"Why don't you just stay there?" Lex suggested. "Let us bring them to you. It'll be quicker."

"I'm all for quick," Jeannie said. "We're running behind."

It wasn't quite what he'd been hoping for when he'd come to the shop but he still got to watch Keely as they handed over trays, catch her smile as they passed. Something about working together created its own intimacy. What he wanted was her and her alone but he was a patient man. After, he'd get her to himself eventually; for now, he'd settle for this.

In truth, he was happy to pitch in. He'd been in Chilton for going on two weeks and he was getting desperate for something to do. Keely had her work at the shop. Olivia had the DAR. He had his camera and that was pretty well it. He'd taken shots of Darlene's shop for her Christmas cards. He'd documented Olivia's house to update her insurance records. He'd taken so many photos of Chilton that he could paper the walls with them.

A couple more days and he was going to go nuts. The time he and Keely weren't together chasing down clues was getting harder and harder to fill.

Or maybe it was just the time without Keely.

The racks were full, trays lined the van floor. And still, there were centerpieces in the shop.

"How many left?" Jeannie asked, climbing out to squeeze in the absolute last tray she could manage.

"Six," Keely reported. "What do you want to do, use the Lexus?" Though she couldn't see how the sedan could take more than three or four of the trays, and even then there would be a substantial risk of one of them tipping over.

Jeannie was already shaking her head. "Much as I hate the idea, we're going to have to do it in two loads. And we're getting way too close to wedding time as it is."

"I've got a better idea." Lex brought out his keys. "Let me bring my Jeep around. We should be able to fit them in there."

"Oh, we couldn't—" Keely began.

"Oh, yes, we could." Jeannie's eyes glimmered with good humor. "We're running way behind. The church is dressed but I still have to bring over the flowers for the entry area and the restrooms at the chapel and the reception hall, both. I'll put in a good word for you with Santa if you can help, Lex. Or pay your gas."

"But—" Keely began.

"Sure." Lex grinned. "I can use all the help with Santa I can get."

"Great." Jeannie walked around to the driver's side of the van. "I'll see you over there."

"Where?" he asked.

"Keely knows." The van's taillights came on as Jeannie started the engine up and then it was pulling away, the Jeannie's Floral Creations logo getting smaller and smaller all the time.

Keely gave him an apologetic shrug as they stepped

back inside. "My mother is sometimes a force of nature."

He grinned. "What mother isn't?"

"You were great to help out but this is way above the call of duty." And the back area felt very small as they stopped by one of the counters. Blossoms rose all around them, the scent enough to dizzy her.

But not nearly so much as Lex did.

"Look, it's not a problem," he said easily. "Let me bring the truck around and we can load up."

"You didn't come here to haul centerpieces," Keely protested. "I'm sure you've got other things to do." She frowned. "Why are you here, anyway? You came here for a reason, right?"

He reached out and brushed his fingertips against the white bells of lily of the valley. "Of course."

"Well, that's what's important. What do you want?"

He looked at her. "You."

It snatched the breath from her lungs. They were fully clothed and yet for a moment, she was as utterly aware of him as though they were lying naked together. Keely swallowed, her throat suddenly dry. "That's not very practical," she managed.

"What's not very practical?"

"You and me."

"After yesterday, I'm not sure I give a damn," he returned.

"What's Stockton going to think if he finds out? And anyway, we've got a job to do. We can't get caught up in…"

"In what?"

They'd started out standing side by side but somehow he'd shifted when she hadn't noticed, so that she was between him and the counter. The sweet scent of lily of the valley rose around them. His eyes were intent, his mouth, so near.

"We didn't really talk about this yesterday." He leaned in closer.

"What is there to talk about? We had sex. I'm not sorry, it was pretty amazing, bu—"

He leaned in to brush his lips over hers. "I'm glad we agree on that. It was pretty amazing. Amazing enough to repeat."

The heat jolted through her. That touch, that merest touch of lip to lip set something vibrating inside her like some bell had been struck. For an instant she could think of only it, and him.

For an instant she could only want.

The door at the front of the shop jingled as a customer came in. The sound of Lydia's voice filtered back to them.

"This isn't the place for this," Keely said unsteadily.

"Then we'll find another one. In the meantime, let's take care of your mother's flowers."

"There's no reason for you to work this project," she told him. And if she had to be around him all night, she might very well find herself giving in to this seductive undertow, like a swimmer going down for the last time.

"Hey, I'm getting benefits out of it. I get points with Santa, I get to do my good deed for the day. And I get to do this."

He pulled her to him for a quick, hard kiss. "I'll do a more thorough job of that later," he promised as he released her and turned away.

And left her there, staring.

* * *

Pathetic, Keely thought as she waited in the alley for Lex. She was pathetic. She had all the good reasons why sleeping together had been a bad thing and was something they shouldn't do again. And then she'd turned around and it had all just melted away in the silly, giddy pleasure of seeing him. The minute he'd walked into the room, all her fine resolutions to give herself time to get her head on straight had gone out the window.

She moistened her lips and tried to ignore the little buzz that the brush of his mouth had set up in her system. It didn't matter that her head had decided she'd be better off keeping her distance. Her body had different plans.

His headlights banished the afternoon shadows in the alley and he pulled up to a stop beside her. And then it was easier to focus on folding down seats, on loading trays, on anything, anything that didn't have to do with his touch, his taste, their pleasure. If she just focused on the logistics at hand, like Hansel and Gretel following the trail of bread crumbs, she could get through this.

Hansel and Gretel had gotten lost, she recalled.

There was something both surreal and wholly ordinary about riding beside Lex again in the Jeep. "Go down Main and make a left at Reservoir," she directed. "You're going to the New Chilton Country Club."

"As opposed to the Chilton Racket and Leisure Club?"

"Exactly."

"The credit reports came," he commented as they sat at one of the town's two stoplights.

That helped change her focus. "And?"

"Nothing out of the ordinary. Olivia reviewed them. They're clean."

"Oh." The disappointment was keen and real. "Well, it was worth a try." She stared out at the shop windows outlined in holiday lights.

"I looked around to see if I could find any clues on the password but no luck."

She shook her head. "This is so frustrating. What we need is on that computer, I know it. And we can't get to it."

"We could take it to a computer doctor."

"And what, tell them that we've lost the password and we've got no proof of ownership and pretty please will they hack into it for us?"

"Okay, so you have a point." Lex made the turn. "Maybe what we should do is call Stockton."

"Not to be a contrarian but only as a last resort. We don't know exactly what's on that computer. If it doesn't hold something to clear us, the last thing we want to do is give him more ammunition. He's still on the lookout for a target, remember?" And the very last thing they needed was for him to suspect a connection between her and Lex. Keely blew out a breath of frustration. "Go right, here."

Turning the other direction would take them to the highway that led to the safe house and the computer and all the questions.

"Is there a chance Bradley might have left something at your place?" Lex asked, following her instructions onto the road that led to the new country club on the outskirts of town.

"The feds sure thought so. That's why they took the place apart."

"I'm not talking about files or records. I mean, could he have hidden a password or something somewhere? I have to go to Manhattan day after tomorrow to meet with one of my wire-service clients. You could come with me and look."

And they could have time and privacy to figure out just what this thing between them was. It probably wasn't smart, it certainly wasn't sensible, but she'd be lying to herself if she said she didn't want it.

"All right," she heard herself saying. "I can't imagine how we'd find anything they didn't, especially after the mess they left, but it couldn't hurt to check." And the thought of what they might do while they checked sent a little curl of desire twisting through her.

"Then tomorrow, it is," Lex said, driving up to the country club's service entrance. "Now, where are we supposed to take these flowers?"

It was the last private moment they had the rest of the afternoon. Keely saw Lex only in passing as Jeannie cheerfully put him to work. Keely caught his quick grin and remembered the taste of his mouth on hers. She watched his arm muscles flex as he moved a marble-topped table in the reception hall and thought of how they'd felt, hard and solid and sweat-slicked under her fingertips.

And as the day wore on, she had to acknowledge the truth of it—she wanted him, pure and simple. She wanted this thing that was between them. Maybe— certainly—it wasn't smart. It didn't matter. No matter how much she tried to intellectualize it, she wasn't going to walk away.

"Well, Lex was certainly a surprise today." Jeannie passed Keely the salad bowl that night as they sat with Carter around the dinner table. "I'll have to do something to thank him."

"I don't think he expects anything." Keely put some greens on her plate. "It's enough that you said it."

Given that she'd decided to abandon her principles and just try to enjoy the present, it was ironic that at twenty-five she was living as though she were in high school. They'd worked until the end of the day, and then Lex had gone back home to Olivia and she'd come home with Jeannie for dinner with her parents. Although there was no reason she couldn't leave after, it wasn't something she'd done before and it would raise questions she wasn't at all sure she wanted to answer. She wasn't at all sure she *could* answer.

And besides, where would they go? To a hotel? To park the car somewhere and make out? And wonder if Stockton's people were watching.

What she wanted was a quiet dinner and a glass of wine with Lex, somewhere peaceful and private. No, that was a lie. What she really wanted was an hour or two of hot, sweaty, wall-banging sex with the man, followed by that quiet dinner, preferably eaten off of his flat, hard belly.

She concentrated on her asparagus, certain she was blushing.

"You and Lex seem to be getting along well. Did I hear you talking about going in to Manhattan tomorrow?" Jeannie asked.

That got her attention. "I wanted to check my apartment, get some clothes, pick up my mail." *Jump his bones.* "Take a look around and see if I can find anything that will help us."

"Didn't the police or whoever already do that?"

"They probably weren't looking for the same thing. They just wanted to seal their case against Bradley. I want to clear Olivia and me."

"Well, good luck. Find something to get my daughter off the hook," Jeannie said lightly.

"We're doing the best we can," Keely replied. And out of nowhere, her throat was suddenly tight. It was tricky like that, the threat, receding out of her consciousness and then catching her unawares. Prosecution. Persecution. Public humiliation. Incarceration.

She blinked.

"Oh, honey," her mother said, rising to put her arms around Keely.

"It's okay, you were joking." She swallowed. "Most of the time I do, too. It's just every so often it all just hits me, where this could lead."

"Where it's going to lead is you being exonerated." Her father squeezed her hand. "You didn't do it and we'll prove it, plain and simple."

His confidence buoyed her. "I hope you're right."

"Of course he is," Jeannie said. "We'll work this out somehow, don't you worry. We know you're innocent and we'll convince them. Now," she said briskly, "don't forget to bring back a gown for the Christmas gala."

Keely blinked at the change in subject. "The gala?"

"The DAR Christmas gala. You have heard of it."

"I unpacked sixty-five cranberry-glass vases yesterday for the centerpieces. I hope I know about it."

"Then you should also know that your father and I buy a table every year. I assumed you'd take one of the places."

Keely looked at her mother as though she'd sprouted two heads. "Why would you go? Why would you want to spend time with those people?"

"You have such a nice, delicate way of saying that," Carter said with amusement.

"Oh, you know what I mean." Her voice was impatient. "Back when we were in financial trouble. All of them, coming to visit, pouring on the fake sympathy while they dug in their claws. The ones who lobbied behind the scenes to get you off their committees since you, God forbid, worked."

"The ones who stood by me," Jeannie countered. "The ones who are still my friends today."

"Alicia Smythe, Joyce Barron, Nancy Pittman. They were horrible. They made you cry."

"Eloise Lucas, Connie Preston. They made me laugh. They still do. They're the ones I go for. No, I don't spend my days in committee meetings anymore but I still support the cause. We still go and we have a lovely time. And if you don't go, people like Alicia Smythe and Joyce Barron will speculate."

"So I'm going to keep them quiet?"

"No, you're going because you'll dance with your father and trade toasts with the Prestons and the Lucases and have a lovely time. What do you think?"

Keely sighed. "I guess I'm bringing home a dress."

Chapter Ten

She dreamed of him.

She was in the store, putting together the Pittman arrangements and Lex appeared through the piles of blossoms. He took her hand without speaking, led her out the back door. Instead of the alley, they walked into a glen filled with mounds of lily of the valley, and suddenly they were pressed together, warm and naked in the sun, while the heady scent of the flowers rose around them. And when he poised his body over hers and made them one, she'd never felt anything so fine.

She dreamed of him and she woke wanting him.

What if there were no Bradley and no Stockton? Lydia had challenged. What if it were really that simple? Could they make it that way? Could they take it on that basis?

Keely showered and dressed and her clothing felt foreign on her body, like the touch of another. She put on her makeup and she thought of his face.

And when she saw him on the doorstep, all she could do was want him.

They didn't touch. They walked to the car without so much as a brush of hands. Outwardly, nothing had changed from two days before. Inwardly, everything was different. Now they weren't wondering how it would be; they knew. Now, they weren't wondering if it would happen; they knew it would.

And despite all the good reasons not to, she wanted it.

They drove to the station, talking little. They watched the trains come and go: to Stamford, to White Plains, to Albany. And still, they didn't touch.

The commuting hour was past. The platform was empty. Somehow it only made her all the more aware of Lex. They stood in the Plexiglas shelter, carefully separate, and Keely swore she could feel the heat from his body radiating through his coat. The minutes crawled by.

It was excruciating.

Keely moistened her lips. She looked at the wires that ran along the track, at the advertisements on the opposite platform, at the wind rattling the bare-branched trees. Down beyond the station, where the track curved away, she saw a train appear. She turned to look at Lex. "Look," she began, "it's—"

He took two steps and fused his mouth with hers.

It wasn't temptation, it wasn't desire. More than anything it was like taking a deep drink of water after days in the desert. Each taste refilled but the need, the thirst had grown to such proportions that it felt like she'd never be slaked. She inhaled his scent, luxuriated in the feel of his arms around her. It was as though the contact of their mouths had some life-giving property, like a magic elixir that could sustain them both.

And she only wanted more. Somewhere private, somewhere quiet, somewhere they could take their time. Somewhere they could start to discover all the possibilities of pleasure.

His tongue danced and darted with hers, he kissed as though he would consume her. The roaring of the blood in her ears became the roar of the train arriving on the platform.

If the minutes had crawled before, now they simply stopped in place. Need pulsed through Keely's veins with every beat of her heart, somehow even more intense now that they weren't touching. She sat beside Lex in the train car, afraid to look at him or speak, afraid that if she did she would simply lose control. It was amazing, after that, how life became defined by waiting: waiting for the train to leave, waiting to get into Grand Central, waiting to get out of the station, waiting to get to her building.

And then they were there, feasting on each other's mouth in the elevator, stopping during the walk down the hall to taste again, and she was at her door, putting the key into the lock with shaking fingers, desperate to get to the bed and privacy that lay just beyond.

She turned the knob and pushed.

"Christ," Lex said.

It was worse than she remembered. In the day and a half she'd stayed in town after the search, she'd focused on trying to deal with her ambiguous legal situation, her job, her life. Her efforts to clear away the mess had only been minor and it showed. The living-room floor was still strewn with cushions and books and dirt from the ficus tree that had been knocked over. She could see into the kitchen, with its mess of spilled dry goods that she hadn't had the heart to clean up.

"Can you take action on them for this?" Lex bent and picked up a handful of CDs, stacking them back in her holder.

"How? They didn't break anything, they just created an unholy mess. It's paralyzing. I don't want to think about it," she said fiercely, pressing her forehead to his chest. "I don't want to see it, I want it just to go away."

I just want you.

And that quickly, the hunger was back. Maybe it was a way of forgetting about what lay around her, maybe it was really about focusing on what mattered. If the apartment hadn't been tossed, they'd have already been naked and in bed. Maybe it was a matter of simply refusing to let events she couldn't control take over.

Two nights, two endless days had passed since they'd made love. Two days had passed and she'd never once stopped thinking about the feel of his body. She'd never once stopped wanting him. It didn't matter that her apartment was torn apart. With her eyes closed, she couldn't see the chaos. With her eyes closed, everything was Lex, everything and all she wanted.

It wasn't gentle. Neither of them wanted gentle. After the seemingly endless wait, the want, the antici-pation, they couldn't go slowly. There would be time later, perhaps, for quiet smoothings and tender caresses, but for now their coupling was hard and fast and urgent.

Feverishly loosening their clothing, they tumbled back on the sofa. It didn't matter that they could have walked to the bedroom, fifteen feet away. There was no time for that, and no patience. There was no time for anything but each other.

With mouth and hand, they touched, they took. When Lex slid his hands up under her sweater, Keely gasped at the suddenness, then made a sound of demand. More and now. Everything and anything. His mouth was on her breast, her hands unbuckled his belt. And when she bent to him, his pleasure was her own.

Time stretched out in a flow of sensation, her mouth on him, his fingers tangled in her hair, the hard immediacy of it all bounding her world, filling it with desire.

And then he stilled her head and hands, dragged her up. Anticipation made her half giddy. She raised her hips to help him strip down her jeans, then lay back beneath his weight, feeling him press her into the deep, soft cushions. She felt, most of all, alive. She was breathless with the expectation and the waiting and the wanting, and then he thrust himself home within her, thick and hard and slick.

And she wasn't waiting anymore.

It was exquisite. It was unbearable. His body surged against hers. Every time he slid home, it dragged a cry from her because it was too intense and too much, and yet somehow not enough. Never enough, she could never have enough as he took her up and up and up until she was suspended in absolute ecstasy, up and up and up until suddenly her body couldn't contain any more. For an endless moment, she was suspended on the edge. And then she tumbled over the edge in an avalanche of pleasure, an overwhelming rush and shudder and swirl that left her shaking as his cries mixed with her own.

Lex didn't want to go, God knew he didn't want to go, but he was here to meet Flaherty, not to make love with Keely, though that was about the best and most important thing he'd done all day, not to say all year.

Kissing her goodbye was hard; walking out the door was harder. And if he didn't watch it, he'd be harder still. "I'll be back in two or three hours," he promised.

"Where are you meeting him?"

"Some bar in the financial district. Don't go away because I've got plans for you." He leaned in to press a kiss on her, lingering more than he'd anticipated.

And throughout the walk and the subway ride, she stayed on his mind, even after he stepped into Flaherty's bar.

It wasn't a bar so much as a watering hole. The long, polished wood that ran down one side bore an assortment of scars and burns. The planked floor was stained. But John Coltrane played on the sound system. The steaks were thick and juicy, the seats, leather and the liquor, top shelf.

Flaherty took a blissful swallow of his whiskey. "Mother's milk." He sighed. "Nothing like a drop o' the Irish to improve the day."

"Where, exactly, did you pick up your taste for the Irish, Flaherty?" Lex asked. "Was that growing up in Philly or after you moved to Poughkeepsie?"

Flaherty frowned at him. "'Tis a sad thing when a man can't get respect."

"I respect you. I'm here, aren't I?"

The waitress set their plates before them. Based on the theory that the thing to order was what a restaurant did well, Lex had chosen steak, like Flaherty. Or not exactly like Flaherty.

"Do you eat that way a lot?" Lex stared at Flaherty's mammoth twenty-ounce London broil.

"When I can. My wife has me on a diet." Flaherty slapped his comfortable paunch. "Worried about cholesterol or some such thing."

"I can see why," Lex said.

It was, he discovered, very good steak, well worth overindulging on. And he wondered immediately if he'd ever be able to really enjoy a meal like this without remembering the things he'd seen in Africa, the hollow eyes, the sunken cheeks, the hopelessness. Some things changed a man forever.

"So how has it been lately, on assignment?" Flaherty inquired, as though he'd known Lex's thoughts.

Lex forced his mind from the topic, a technique at which he'd grown increasingly skilled. "The same, only more so. Some days better than others. Why? Where do you want me to go?"

"I've been looking at your shots," Flaherty said instead of answering.

"You got a problem with my shots?"

"No. They're top quality. I'd pick your stuff over anybody else's any day, you know that."

"But?"

"But when I talk to you lately, you sound like you're losing your edge." He bit into a steak fry.

"Give me a break, Flaherty. I've been in Chechnya,

the Gaza Strip, Baghdad and Darfur. It hasn't exactly been a holiday camp this year."

"Or last year."

Lex scowled. "I've already got a mother."

"Who might be happy to see you stick around for a while. Maybe you should take a break."

"You're supposed to be a client, not a career coach."

"Maybe I'm just a friend."

"I'm freelance, Flaherty. I can't take a break."

"You could if you took on a salaried job."

"Ah." The bait, Lex thought, was out. "Can you hand me the steak sauce?" he asked.

Flaherty passed it over. "Since you're obviously dying of curiosity, I'll tell you that I'm taking a one year sabbatical. I've had a book project I've always wanted to do. The time's right. I need to leave the desk in good hands, though. The problem is, there's no one in the organization whose eye I trust. I want you to take over the desk for a year."

Lex took a bite of his sirloin and chewed. "Good steak," he commented after swallowing. "Done just right. How's yours?"

"You're not asking me about the job."

"I'm asking about your steak. Good sauce, too. You think they make this here?" He took another bite.

"You'd be good at it, you know you would."

Lex let his fork drop to the plate with a clink. "I've got three other clients, Joe. International outlets. What am I supposed to do with them in the meantime?"

"We'd make it worth your while. Bring you on in a salaried position, full bennies. Who knows, if it works out, it could turn into a long-term thing."

"Until you come back."

"If." Flaherty held up his whiskey and inspected it. "*If* is the operative word. I'm fifty-eight. It's time to start thinking about what comes next. This book thing is a trial run. We'll see where it goes."

"You'd have a lot better luck getting me to say yes if you made it a contract job."

"I'll take my chances." He switched his gaze to Lex. "I want you in the organization. You belong there. With what you know, you could make a big difference."

"I do that in the field."

"This is just a different way of doing it. You need the right touch after the photo's taken, as well as before, if you want it to have the impact you intended. Will you at least think about it? Tell me you'll do that much."

"I'll think about it," Lex told him, with the feeling of the sand slipping beneath his feet.

Being back in Manhattan was supposed to feel familiar, comforting. Keely couldn't figure out why it didn't. Instead, it felt strange, stifling—too many hurried people, too much concrete, maybe. Too much noise. And yet, she'd only been gone for a couple of weeks. Why, then, did she feel so much at loose ends, so disconnected?

She'd gotten serious about cleaning up after Lex had gone, picking up, sweeping, vacuuming until some order began to emerge. As it did, some of the tension she felt began to abate. A glance around no longer slapped her in the face with the knowledge that strangers had invaded every corner of her home. Now it was low-grade, background anxiety.

But it was still there.

She'd searched everywhere to find some trace of Bradley, some clue about a password. There was no cryptic slip of paper tucked in a drawer, no writing on the wall with circles and arrows. She worked and thought about Bradley and scribbled down a few possibilities, but nothing she wanted to stake her future on.

So she put Norah Jones on the stereo instead and sang along, tossing a couple of shirts and sweaters, and some jeans into her overnight bag. She was sick and tired of wearing the same thing.

She was also sick and tired of cleaning. There was so much to do yet, and she hadn't even started on the corner of her bedroom that she used as an office only gathered the strewn-about papers into an untidy stack. She should keep at it. Instead, she pulled out a gown for the gala and put it into a dress bag.

When Lex rang the bell, she buzzed him in and waited expectantly as he walked through the door.

"Wow," he said as he looked around.

"Wow good or wow bad?"

"Wow, you've gotten a lot done." He turned to her. "Wow, it looks better." He slid an arm around her waist. "Wow, I really like your mouth," he murmured, leaning in and browsing on it until she felt warmth spreading through her. They sank down to the floor together.

A long while later, Keely stirred.

"Where are you going?"

"We can't just lay around here all day having sex," she moved to rise, reaching for her clothing.

"Sure we can." He reached for her. "Let me show you."

"No," she said firmly, picking her sweater off the floor, "we have to get the train home."

"We've got until at least eleven. Or we could stay."

She thought longingly of spending the night with him, just the two of them. "There's Stockton. And my parents. I'm not sure I'm ready to deal with the questions." Because it would mean facing things she wasn't ready to just yet. How could she explain what she was doing to her mother when she didn't fully understand it herself? Because Jeannie *would* figure it out. Keely had only Nancy Pittman and her lily of the valley to thank for the fact that Jeannie hadn't noticed already.

And once she did, she'd have her daughter's head examined. Assuming her daughter hadn't already decided to do it on her own. But, oh, if she knew where Lex could take Keely with those hands, that mouth, Jeannie would understand.

Keely sighed. "We really have to go," she said.

"I guess you're right." Lex rose and pulled on his jeans, trailing after her into her bedroom to watch as she finished her packing.

"Do you see the charger for my BlackBerry anywhere?" she asked, poking around her desk and bureau.

Lex picked up a framed photograph that was leaning against the wall. "Does this go here?" He nodded to a hook.

Keely took the picture from him and turned it over. White sails, blue water. She and Bradley grinned out at the camera from their seats near the tiller of his boat. They'd taken the shot on Labor Day weekend a year before, just after they'd gotten engaged. His arm was around her shoulders; her hands were on his. In his tanned, sun-bleached smile, Keely searched for some hint of the mess that he'd already made of both of their lives. In her own expression there was only uncomplicated joy.

She didn't recognize that person, the woman who had faced the world with trust. How could she, she who knew better? How had she let herself get fooled, dropped into a desperate situation with less and less hope of escape? "What a sap," she muttered, and dropped the photo into the trash can.

She looked around the room, swiping her hair out of her face.

"You okay?" Lex asked.

"I'm just looking for my iPod," she said, turning back to the desk and its island of chaos.

"Hey," he said.

"My iPod," she said desperately. "It's one of the little ones. Blue." She couldn't bear for him to be kind just then. Stupidity had its punishment; she'd just gotten it a bit more than most.

"I don't see it," Lex said, picking up books, moving papers around. "I saw a blue one at the house. Could Brad have borrowed it without telling you?"

"I don't see why not. He didn't tell me about anything else." Her throat tightened. It was one more thing. It was all too much.

"It doesn't matter," she said, blinking fiercely. Nothing mattered. And she was getting sick, so sick of having meltdowns around Lex. She grabbed her bag and walked out of the room.

"Hey." He caught up with her and turned her around. "He didn't deserve you."

"It's not that." Keely stopped. "I'm not usually a basket case," she began.

"I know."

"That's the problem," she burst out. "You don't know. All you've seen is me being a mess. I'm not usually like this."

"I do know," he said steadily. "I saw this place this morning, remember? I'm amazed that you've held together as well as you have."

"I just…" She let out a long, slow breath. "I can't believe I bought it all. I look at that picture and there's me, all smiley, dumb and happy. And there's Bradley. He had the whole scheme in place back then. He was working with Skele, probably already sleeping around. He was doing it all and I didn't have a clue."

He traced a finger along her jaw. "It's not a crime to trust."

"It's dangerous, though." She looked at him soberly. "I can't even trust myself. I don't know who to trust, what to trust anymore."

"Trust this," he whispered, and fastened his mouth over hers.

They lay in bed together, the sheets twined around them, the sun long gone. Lovemaking had left Keely's limbs heavy with sleepy languor. They needed to go home, she knew that, but somehow she couldn't quite make it matter. Instead, she lay with her head pillowed on Lex's chest.

"So tell me about you," she asked.

"Like what?"

"Like how did you get into photography?"

His fingertips trailed down over her back in soft, hypnotic strokes. "My grandmother. She gave me a camera for my birthday. I was eleven. I couldn't get enough of it. Spent all my allowance on developing and film."

"Your allowance?"

"Pierce was big on teaching us financial responsibility. It was part of his grand scheme to turn us into management material."

"I'm guessing he wasn't big on the photography."

Lex laughed in genuine amusement. "He wanted to see me saving my allowance, not blowing it on artsy-fartsy crap."

"His words?"

"Oh, yeah. He was a baby boomer but he wasn't exactly one of those actualize yourself hippie types. He was more into self-actualization in the boardroom."

She couldn't imagine anything less well suited to Lex. "I guess the two didn't square with each other."

"Not as he saw it." Lex kissed her hair. "Not as I saw it, either. I didn't want his world. From the time I was a kid, he had this really clear vision of who and what I should be, no ifs, ands or buts."

"You were a person, not a piece of clay," she murmured, raising her head to look into his eyes.

"No, I was Aubrey Pierce Alexander III and I had a responsibility to the family and the company. Choice didn't enter into it. The photography stuff he saw as rebellion. It drove him nuts, especially because I was screwing around in my classes. Photography was the only one I liked. That, I aced. Best in class, awards, the whole deal."

"You won an award?" she asked, delighted. "For what?"

"Best nature study, I think. It was a picture of the brook in winter."

"That should have done something to change his mind."

"Oh, it did. He yanked me from the school and enrolled me in a prep school that advertised its discipline—and that didn't have any art programs."

"What did you do?"

Lex shrugged. "A few things I shouldn't have. Got mouthy with some of the teachers. They weren't the ones I was angry at but I was fourteen and they were trying to force feed me supply-side economics. I was bored, so I pulled some stupid stunts."

"Sneaking out of the dorms?"

"Sneaking into some classrooms. Letting loose all the animals in the biology labs, loosening the screws on teachers' lounge doorknob so that they all got locked inside at break, that sort of thing. When they'd had enough, they booted me out."

"What did Pierce do?"

The corners of his mouth curved faintly. "Sent me off to a military academy. I got really good at doing pushups." The smile held no humor. "By then I was six-teen and nothing was going to change my mind. Pierce lectured me that I wasn't applying myself to my goals. Or his goals, rather. On my goals, I did fine. It's sur-prisingly hard to get kicked out of military school, but I managed it three times. By the time we ran out of academies, I was almost eighteen."

Keely stroked her fingers down his cheek. "I heard

rumors. You came home that summer, I remember seeing you." Tall, dark, brooding. He'd shown up in the middle of a tennis match she'd been playing with Bradley. Looking back, she wondered how she'd ever missed the tension between the two brothers.

"I was back that summer, but not for long."

The mother of all fights, according to Bradley, though he'd been sketchy on the details. Lex's first brush with the law, or so Bradley had said. Keely wondered. "So what really happened?" she asked.

"I think Pierce had given up on making me into who he wanted, by then. It had come down to a battle of wills. It was the day before my birthday. One of his control games was to keep me without a car, but my buddies and I wanted to go out. I asked if I could use one of the cars and he told me no. So I took it without permission."

"What did he do?"

"He was buddies with the sheriff, so he had me hauled in and held overnight. Happy birthday, son."

"My God." She stared.

"Once I got out, I went looking for him. Half an hour later, I was walking out to I-95 with my cameras and my passport and the clothes I had on me."

Eighteen and angry. And probably scared to death. "Oh, Lex," she whispered.

"It's okay. It was a long time ago. Pierce is gone, things worked out."

"And you're back home."

"Back in Chilton," he corrected. "Not home."

"Are you sure of that?"

He looked at her for a long time. "It's different than

I remember. I don't know if it's because there's no Pierce or that it's changed. Or that I have."

"You're different than I remember," she said.

"What do you remember?"

"Surly, brooding. Hostile. Bradley always said you were trouble."

His lips twitched. "I am trouble."

"You did a good job of looking like it. You always made me a little uncomfortable." More than a little, she remembered, but maybe it hadn't been uncomfortable at all. Maybe it had been some part of her recognizing the first stirrings of the attraction that would exist between them, an attraction she had been in no way ready to face at fourteen.

"I remember you, always in your tennis skirt, always with your hair brushed. You're different than I remember, too." Mischief glimmered in his eyes. "The girl I knew was headed for the Junior League and a lifetime of fancy lunches."

"Funny what happens when you lose your money." Her tone was flippant.

"My mom told me about that," he said quietly. "I'm sorry."

"Don't be. We survived and I think my parents are happier for it."

"What about you?"

"I survived, too."

"How old were you when it happened?"

"A junior in high school." She rolled onto her back. "My dad spent his time back then just managing our money. He did well during the bubble with day trading. Then again, everyone did. When the bottom dropped out, it was awful." She swallowed. "I remember coming home every day to worse and worse news until I started to dread walking through the door. Just the atmosphere was toxic. Eventually, he wouldn't even come out of his office, just stayed there all night doing after hours trading and trying to get ahead."

"Like trying to gamble your way back from a loss."

"Kind of," she agreed. "It was brutal. In a way, it was almost best when everything hit rock bottom and stayed there. When he finally gave up, that was when he was able to start the recovery."

Lex stroked her hair. "It must have been tough on you."

She remembered the strain in the faces of her parents. She remembered weeping over the sale of the chateau in Provence where they'd spent August for as long as she could remember. She remembered the friends who'd melted away, talking about trips and things that were no longer a part of her world.

Like Lara and the friends who'd melted away in New York.

"It wasn't the money and things, so much," she said slowly. "What was hardest was that everything changed." Her place in the world, in her community, was different. The security she'd always taken for granted was suddenly gone, and if that could happen, what could she depend upon? "For as long as I could remember, things just were. I trusted that. And then it all fell apart beneath me. Like stepping on granite and finding quicksand."

Like with Bradley, she realized in sudden shock.

"Did I mention," Lex said casually, "that my brother

is a punk?" His gaze was steady on hers. "Since he's not here to say it, and probably wouldn't if he were, I'll say it for him—I'm sorry. I'm sorry for what he's done and what he's put you through."

She stared at him, and suddenly it was as though every line of his face assumed some special importance. Suddenly his gaze seemed to widen to encompass her entire universe. Time and breath stopped, as though the two of them existed between ticks of the clock, between worlds, between heartbeats. And the knowledge shivered through her, solid and undeniable.

She was in love with him.

Chapter Eleven

"You don't have to do this, you know." Darlene stared at Keely across the bakery counter, exasperated.

"I know I don't have to. I want to. I can do it faster than you can and quite frankly, it's in my own best interest. You might forget about it or mess it up and the IRS will come haul you off in shackles and then where will I be? A cruller junkie without a supplier." Keely folded her arms in imitation of Darlene. "I'm not leaving here until you let me into your office. Unless you're worried about the legal thing."

"I'm not worried about the legal thing."

"Then deal with it."

Darlene rolled her eyes. "All right, all right. Come on in."

Keely skirted the counter and walked through the

swinging door that led into the bakery itself. "You know, in all the years I've been coming here, I don't think I've ever made it into the back," she commented as they passed the white counters and the wall of ovens. One of Darlene's assistants turned a cake on a rotating pedestal while she spread on chocolate frosting with a long, thin spatula. Another pulled a pan of muffins from the oven. "I didn't know you had elves. I thought you did it all by magic."

"There are only so many crullers one woman can make," Darlene said. "I had to hire help to keep up with you."

"I can see how that might be."

They stopped before open door on the far wall of the room. "Okay, brace yourself," Darlene said as she flipped on the light. "Welcome to my lair."

It was more closet than office, with barely enough room for a desk, a chair and a green plastic trash can. Notes on orders and ship dates covered an oversized wall calendar. On a white board, Darlene had inked the week's staffing schedule. An old fashioned monitor and keyboard sat on the desk, amid teetering stacks of paperwork.

Darlene leaned down and flipped on the CPU. "The printer's behind the desk. I've got basic accounting and payroll software." She clicked to start the program and punched in the password. "The file the accountant gave me is right here. You want coffee?"

"Yes, please," Keely said.

"Be right back."

Keely pulled out the chair and opened the file to begin reviewing the payroll documents that she knew by heart. It wasn't just that she wanted to help Darlene or to keep busy; she was glad to have something to focus on because she was spending way too much time dwelling on Lex.

She'd fallen in love with him. Bad enough she was sleeping with him but, no, she'd gone for the big kahuna. What in God's name was she thinking of? She'd fallen in love with a man who had no known address. Whose places of work generally featured AK-47s and shoulder-mounted missile launchers. Who was in town only to take care of his mother's legal problems and who evinced every desire to leave immediately thereafter.

And despite all that, despite her better judgment, she'd gotten hung up on him. Not just hung up. In love. The big "*L.*"

"Great, Stafford. Brilliant," she muttered. Fall in love with a guy who was never around, who spent his time on assignment dodging bullets. Hadn't the fiasco with Bradley taught her anything? Hadn't she learned better than to get herself tangled up with another Alexander?

And yet being with Lex felt so right.

Like she knew anything about it, she thought, punching in numbers bad temperedly. She'd been sure it was love with Bradley, too, solidly, rock-hard sure of it, and she'd been wrong. Who was to say this was any different? Maybe she just confused lust with love. Except that it had never been lust with Bradley, but something less, and it wasn't just lust with Lex, but something much more.

Or was it? Once the situation was corrected, once

they were no longer on a desperate search for vindication, would that strange link between them still exist? Or would they just be two people who had scratched a momentary itch with one another?

Keely sighed and picked up the coffee Darlene had left on the desk. Lydia would probably tell her to go with it. Keely wasn't sure she had a choice. It wasn't smart, it probably wasn't healthy. It simply was. She loved him and she couldn't just stop because she wanted to. Yes, she was setting herself up to get hurt, without a doubt, because he was leaving. Without a doubt.

And all she could really do was enjoy the time they had.

Keely stabbed viciously at the enter key and the printer began to hum.

"You got home late last night," Olivia observed at the breakfast table, stirring her tea.

Lex glanced over. "It's true." Not by his choice. All things considered, he'd have preferred to spend the night with Keely, to wake with her in the morning. But she'd wanted to get home and there was little he could do but respect that. He couldn't blame her for not wanting to face a lot of questions about their involvement. Given the Bradley connection, it would raise more than a few eyebrows.

In the case of Olivia, it would more likely raise hell.

So maybe discretion was the ticket for now but he wasn't crazy about it. He'd given up trying to live by other people's rules and standards the day he'd walked away from Chilton. Since then, he'd taken his lumps for various interesting screw-ups but he'd kept his promise to himself to be what he was and who he was.

An ongoing struggle since he'd returned.

"Your father's tuxedo came back from the tailor's yesterday." Olivia spooned up some of her boiled egg. "Be sure to try it on as early as possible to make sure the alterations are all right."

"I'm sure it'll be fine."

"But how can you be? If something needs fixing, there's still time this morning. By afternoon, it'll be too late. We'll need to leave for the gala at around three."

Lex resisted the urge to protest. If she needed him to help her at the gala, she needed him to help her at the gala.

The Christmas gala was the event of the town social season, an annual holiday gathering for some five hundred of the Chilton glitterati. Ostensibly, it was a fundraiser for cancer research and the local medical center, but it was as much as anything a see-and-be-seen event.

As chair, Olivia worked for the better part of the year to pull it all together. It was a holiday bash for a good cause. Hard to be too down on it.

He just wished he could get out of going.

But Olivia needed an escort and with Bradley gone, it fell to Lex once again to step into his father's shoes—in this case literally. He knew all the reasons for it, but it still made him chafe. Just as he knew that it was the emotional upheaval that Olivia had been through—losing her husband, being betrayed by her son—that made her so dependent on him.

It was still suffocating.

He could only hope that something on the list of possible passwords Keely had compiled would get them into Bradley's machine. They could get the information, clear Olivia and Keely, and duty would be discharged. The threat to Olivia would be gone and Lex's life could go back to normal. Before he went nuts.

Before he got in too deep to walk away.

"Okay," he said. "You want to be there at three, we'll be there."

Small, Chilton might have been, but it was one of the wealthiest enclaves in Connecticut—indeed, in the country—and it had a country club to match.

Two of them, actually, but the one that really counted, the only one, was the Chilton Racket and Leisure Club. Built in 1902, the Club, as it was simply known, sprawled across three hundred acres of rolling terrain with emerald golf courses, woods, tanbark riding trails and red clay courts. Its membership was among the most exclusive in New England. It was rumored that some of the biggest Wall Street acquisitions and mergers over the past century had been negotiated from the deep, leather club chairs around the tables in the bar.

Now a long line of vehicles snaked up the hill to the Palladian-style clubhouse. Designed by a famous architect, the sprawling pale limestone building glowed like a beacon. Light blazed from the enormous windows. Holiday garland swagged the facade. Black-jacketed valets dashed back and forth, spiriting away Rolls Royces, Jaguars, Bentleys and Mercedes.

Keely stepped on the red carpet with a sense of unreality. It had been years since she'd been to the Club.

Growing up, she'd practically lived there in the summers with her tribe of friends, playing tennis, splashing in the pools, gleefully slicing balls at the driving range, exhausting the saddle horses on the trails.

When the money had gone, they'd given up their membership. It had felt like being excommunicated. Abruptly, she was on the outside looking in, the pleasures she'd taken as part of her world suddenly denied. As a girl, she'd never thought twice about being in a place where every need was anticipated and every request instantly served. Learning that it wasn't the real world had been a hard lesson. Her parents had joined up again as of a few years ago and her card once again gave her free rein, but she'd never been back. It was different, somehow.

"Good evening, Mr. and Mrs. Stafford." The tuxedoed greeter nodded at them as they stepped over the threshold. A smiling woman in a black skirt and jacket spirited away their coats. "The gala is in the main ballroom."

There was something about walking into the ballroom that held an air of expectancy, as though she were walking into another world. It wasn't just an ordinary door but a gracefully curving archway. Inside, the ceiling soared high overhead, carrying away the hubbub of several hundred people all talking at once. The carpet was plush underfoot. A staggering number of tables filled the space.

Sixty-five of them, to be exact. Keely could say that with confidence because she and Jeannie and Lydia had arranged and transported centerpieces for all of them, as well as the floral cascades around the stage and in the entryway. That afternoon, when they'd put the flowers in place, the light had been mercilessly bright, the tablecloths bare. Now, china and silver gleamed and the enormous chandeliers cast a soft glow over the pale shoulders of jewel-bedecked women. In the corner, an orchestra played "Winter Wonderland."

"Smile," Jeannie murmured into her ear, handing her a canapé from the tray of a passing waiter. "You're having fun."

And somehow, Keely found herself with a champagne glass in hand, smiling and nodding at people she'd known since she'd been a child.

"Well, Keely Stafford, aren't you a picture?" an older man with a shock of white hair said to her. "And here alone. The young men don't have two brain cells among them, these days, do they? Why, if I were forty years younger, I'd take you and run off to Monte Carlo." He gave her a roguish wink.

"Isn't that your wife coming, Mr. Lucas?" Keely said, fighting a smile.

"Oh, right. Mum's the word. Hello, Eloise," he said to the beaming silver haired woman in lavender who walked up beside him.

"Hello, dear," she said. "Have you been asking Keely to run away with you again?"

"I think this is going to cost me a diamond necklace," he whispered to Keely.

Eloise patted his hand. "A nice orange tree for the solarium will do, dear. And a turn or two around the dance floor."

"Only as long as Keely saves a dance for me," he said.

"Oh, you must, Keely, or I'll never hear the end of it," Eloise said, rolling her eyes. "Come along, Ben, the Prestons are here."

"Didn't we just see them yesterday?" he muttered aggrievedly.

"Yes, dear, but now it's tonight."

"Don't forget about that dance," he warned Keely as Eloise tugged him away.

Keely laughed at his hangdog look and began to enjoy herself.

"Careful," Jeannie whispered. "You're smiling."

The Christmas gala was all the things about the Chilton lifestyle that Lex loathed. He knew how much of the money raised at these events went to cover the food, the presentation, the entertainment, and how little ever made it to the designated charities.

It was the last place he wanted to be.

But he stood in his father's tux alongside Olivia, resisting the urge to tug at his collar like a small boy. So he wasn't in the habit of being anyone's lackey. It was his mother, not just anyone, and it was Christmas. It was little enough to do.

Except that he had the uneasy feeling that it wasn't just a Christmas thing. Olivia was more subtle than Pierce, but in her own way, she was trying to push Lex into that same box. Somehow, he'd become her escort, her accountant, her financial advisor, her investigative assistant. If she had her way, soon enough he'd be her board representative.

"You remember my son Trey, don't you?" Olivia was saying to an emaciated woman with a designer dress and the permanently surprised expression of a facelift veteran. "Trey, you remember Alicia Smythe."

He dredged up a smile and held out his hand obediently. "Hello, Mrs. Smythe."

She gave him the countess squeeze that a certain sort of woman considered a handshake. "Alicia, please," she said. "Trey, how good to see you again. You certainly look like things have been going well for you." Her eyes gleamed. "I understand you've been working, ah, import/export overseas."

Bradley, Lex thought, had been busy. "Actually, I'm a photographer."

"How nice for you," she said insincerely, ignoring his words. "And, Olivia, how's that other son of yours? He got loose from that Stafford girl, I understand. None too soon, if you ask me."

That Stafford girl.

The woman's voice lowered. "They're here tonight, if you can believe it. Just walk in as big as life every year as though they had a right to. As though they still belonged."

That did it. Lex opened his mouth.

"Isn't that a lovely necklace you have on, Alicia," Olivia interrupted before he could say a word. "Wherever did you get it?"

"Oh, this old thing?" The Smythe woman patted it as though to remember which one she was wearing. "I stopped by Harry Winston last time I was out in Beverly Hills. It's so hard to find good emeralds. Why, I was just telling Joyce the other day—"

"Excuse me," Lex broke in. "I need to go hunt down another drink."

What he needed was to get out of there before the top of his head blew off. "That Stafford girl." The silky condescension in Smythe's voice had him gritting his teeth. What was Olivia doing spending time with these people? What was he? They were insipid, shallow, mean-spirited. They were wastes of time.

The only even remotely pleasant or useful bit of the whole discussion was the news that Keely and her family were there. He'd known Jeannie was doing the flowers for the event. Keely hadn't talked about coming. Instantly, the night began to look up.

Casually, he navigated the edges of the ballroom, smiling, nodding, never stopping, looking always for the one person who could make the night worthwhile.

And then he saw her.

She was, simply, beautiful. Amid all the rainbow drama of fabrics and jewels, she had chosen simplicity. Her gown was cut like that of a Grecian goddess, draping from the shoulders and falling to her feet in a waterfall of silken white, leaving her arms bare. Gold gleamed—at her ears and throat, in a cuff around one of her narrow wrists that made it look almost unbearably fragile. Her hair was pulled up in a complicated plait that focused the eye on her slender neck.

And on her face. She was luminous, as though she radiated light from inside. Did he see it because she was his? he wondered. Because he knew what it was to watch her expression slip from pleasure into ecstasy while he was inside her?

But then her eyes lit and she smiled at someone past him and he found himself taking an involuntary breath. She smiled and walked directly toward him and all he could do was wonder how the hell he'd gotten so lucky as to be standing in this particular spot at this particular time.

And totally unaware of him, she passed by to go to a white-haired gentleman. "Someone promised me a dance," she was saying. "I'm going to collect, Mr. Lucas, that's all there is to it."

With a bow, Lucas held out his arm. "A dance you want and a dance you shall have."

Bemused, Lex watched the pair go to the floor. With great seriousness, Lucas held up his hands in dance position. Keely stepped in and they began to move in a slow, formal waltz.

It was the first time Lex had really ever been able to watch her when she was unawares. It was the first time he'd seen her without the threat of the future hanging over her. Her eyes sparkled, her laugh was infectious. She was long and lovely in her fluid gown. She and her partner rose and dipped to the music, moving in and out of the shadows thrown by the chandeliers. And as they circled the floor, Lex felt a sweet twist inside him.

The song drew to an end and Lucas twirled Keely around to a stop at the edge of the floor and bowed. "Thank you, my dear, for a lovely, lovely dance."

"Thank you," Keely said, leaning in to kiss him on the cheek.

And Lex couldn't wait any longer. "May I cut in?" he asked, stepping forward.

Keely's eyes seemed to grow larger as their gazes met. Her lips parted, and it damned near took his breath away. "Of course," she murmured.

The white-haired guy squinted at him. "Cutting in?"

"If you're done."

He gave Lex an assessing look and then nodded. "Okay by me. This one appears to have a brain," he added to Keely.

"Oh, he does," Keely assured him, laughter in her eyes.

"Should I know what that was about?" Lex asked as he pulled her into his arms.

"I don't think so. Merry Christmas," she added as the orchestra began to play "Tennessee Waltz."

"Merry Christmas to you. Are you having a good time?"

"Surprisingly, yes. Are you?"

She was featherlight in his arms. He caught a hint of her scent. "I am now."

Her smile was brilliant. "Smooth talker."

"You're beautiful," he said before he knew he was going to.

Keely missed a step and lurched against him for an instant. "Definitely a smooth talker." But she didn't laugh.

In the soft lighting, her eyes were dark and enormous. The chandeliers threw shadows across the fragile curves of her collar bones. Her mouth mesmerized him. "I want to kiss you," he said.

"We can't."

"I still want to. I think I may always want to." He'd intended it as a quip but somehow as he said it, he realized it was true. In this moment, at this time, he couldn't ever imagine being with any other woman. It was Keely, all he needed, all he wanted. No one else mattered. No one else ever could.

Like stepping on granite and having it turn to quicksand, she'd once said to him.

Him, the loner, the guy who never got carried away. Him, the guy who knew what he wanted and where he was going. He'd stepped on solid ground, it had turned to water under his feet. And suddenly he found himself in over his head.

In over his head and scared as hell.

Chapter Twelve

The snow crunched underfoot as Lex walked down the road. His breath formed white plumes in the morning air. He hunched his shoulders in his jacket and ignored the cold. It felt too good to be outside and moving.

He'd been up at dawn, restless and edgy, feeling itchy in his own skin. If he'd still been on the rhino assignment, he'd have been hiking in to the blind near the watering hole, hoping to hide out and catch the poachers in the act of setting their snares. He'd be focused on action and activity and the work that made his life worthwhile.

But he wasn't on assignment, he wasn't working. He was just spinning his wheels in Chilton, feeling stuck deeper in the mud with each passing day. And so he found himself out on the roads, walking next to the snow banks, proving to himself that he wasn't completely immobile.

And he was full of it because he knew damned good and well that no matter how far he walked, he wasn't going to get away from what was really eating at him.

What the hell was wrong with him? He had no business getting serious about Keely Stafford. It was one thing to have a quick affair, to take and give pleasure. It was another to let her get inside his head. It was foolish to let emotions enter into it. And it would be even more of a mistake to start thinking about a future with her.

A mistake for both of them.

The door to Darlene's jingled as he stepped inside, stomping the snow off his boots. Caffeine was probably the last thing he needed but until something better came along, it would have to do.

It was early enough that the shop was still empty. Darlene bustled out from the back. "Merry Christmas," she sang out. "Nine more shopping days. Better head to the mall now."

"Coffee," he growled.

She raised a brow. "Sounds like someone got up on the wrong side of the bed this morning."

His reply was interrupted by the ring of his cell phone.

"You going to answer that?" Darlene asked.

Lex shot her a sharp look. He hadn't brought the phone intentionally. It was only in his jacket pocket because it had been there the day before, a result of Olivia's campaign to get him to carry it all the time. He was in no mood to talk with anyone. For that matter,

he couldn't even figure who might be calling him.
Still…

Reluctantly, he pulled out the phone, to see
Flaherty's number on the display. Fighting the urge to
curse, Lex snapped the phone open. "You want to tell
me why you're bugging me on a Sunday morning?"

"I thought I'd call and see if you had any sins you
wanted to confess, me lad."

"Father forgive me, for I'm contemplating stran-
gling someone."

"And who would that be?"

"You."

Flaherty laughed. "Did I interrupt your beauty
sleep? I was just calling to see if you'd had any time to
think about our discussion."

"It's been three days, Flaherty. I've barely gotten
home from the train station." Even he could hear the
edge in his voice.

"I just thought if you had any questions, I could answer them."

Lex stared at an old photo of barnstormers posing
with their planes. "Yeah, I've got a question. Can you
give me some room to breathe here?"

"Well, well, well," Flaherty said slowly, the amusement replaced by satisfaction.

"What have you got to be so smug about?"

"I know you, Lex, my boy, and if you'd already decided against the job, you'd be telling me to take a hike
right now."

"Is that a dare?"

"Just an observation. The point is, you're not turning
it down." The whisper of triumph in his voice rankled.

And for the life of him, Lex couldn't figure what was preventing him from telling Flaherty what he could do with both his observations and his job.

"This is good news," Flaherty continued blithely. "I think you're weakening. Have a good rest of your weekend, laddie. My best to your mother. And we'll be talking again, soon."

"Go choke on a waffle." Lex cut off the call and snapped the phone closed.

Darlene stared at him, wide-eyed. "Remind me never to call you on a Sunday morning," she said.

"It's just a guy bugging me about a job."

"Well, I'm sure you're going to get it, you charmer."

"I don't want it." Flaherty—yet another person trying to back him into a corner.

"What's the job?"

"Working as a desk jockey for a wire service in New York next year."

Her eyes gleamed. "Do tell."

"No, if you don't mind, I won't."

"If you don't want the job, why didn't you just say so?" she asked, stacking fresh-baked corn muffins in the display case.

Lex glowered at her. "Don't you have anything better to do than eavesdrop on customers' phone calls?"

"Kind of hard not to when they're three feet in front of me," she said mildly. "And I noticed you didn't say no to him. I'm just saying. As an old friend."

Lex leaned toward her, planting his hands on the countertop for leverage. "Hey, Darlene? As an old friend—I've got enough stuff on my mind right now without one more person putting pressure on me. Now, can I get that coffee?"

Darlene eyed him speculatively as she reached for the coffeepot. "The world is full of pressure these days, isn't it? Particularly the kind of pressure you get from blond hair and gray eyes, nice figure, good family…" As his eyes narrowed, she laughed. "I'm not blind, Lex, though it seems like the rest of this town might be. I see how you two look at each other. You've got good taste. And despite your present crankiness, so does she."

Great, he was becoming obvious. His immediate impulse was to tell Darlene she was wrong, but one look into her eyes took the fight out of him.

"Let's not talk about this right now, okay?" he muttered.

Darlene smiled slightly and set his coffee on the counter between his hands. "Maybe this will help. Try some sugar, it'll sweeten things up."

She turned to the wall behind her and pulled out a pushpin to take down a postcard. She'd already cleared away at least half of them, he saw.

"You got someone else sending you postcards?"

She shrugged. "The wall was full. I figured I'd take some down to make some more room. Of course, now I'm starting to think maybe I should put them in a scrapbook. I get the feeling you might be sticking around."

"No way."

"Don't dismiss the idea so fast. It's been nice having you around. I'm not the only one who thinks so."

And again he could feel the potential entanglements

snatching at him, as if his sleeve had been caught by the gears of a giant machine, the one he'd escaped at eighteen. His mother, Flaherty, Darlene. Even Keely. People all around him suddenly wanted things from him, to have him become yet another cog spinning in one place that would make the world this town represented run more smoothly.

Lex placed a dollar carefully on the counter and picked up the steaming paper cup Darlene had set before him. "Go ahead and clear that wall. I'll send you enough new postcards to cover it twice." He turned and left the shop, the bell above the door jangling again as it closed behind him.

Sunlight slanted through the stained glass windows at the side of the church. The voices of the choir filtered down from above them like the song of angels. Incense scented the air.

Keely always found services at her childhood church soothing. So maybe she was well and truly lapsed, and maybe she guided her life these days by her own moral compass rather than the teachings of the High Episcopalian church, but there was something about sitting on the polished wood pew next to her parents and listening to the drone of Reverend Richards' voice that soothed.

And on this day, of all days, she could use soothing.

She wasn't upset exactly. She wasn't even quite on edge. She was just…unsettled. Something wasn't quite right. She couldn't say how she knew it but she knew it, as though she were walking across a railroad trestle and feeling the first distant hint of an oncoming train in the tiny vibrations of the track.

She turned her head slightly to stare at the stained glass window that showed the Annunciation. She didn't need archangels appearing with trumpets to tell her what was going on; she'd have settled for a whisper.

"Don't gawk," Jeannie chided sotto voce, just as she had when Keely had been a girl.

Now, as then, Keely listened to the Reverend's voice and let her thoughts spiral away, and suddenly she was back at the gala, warm with the fizz of champagne, circling the dance floor in Lex's arms.

All little girls, she guessed, dreamed of being a fairy princess in the arms of a prince. And for those few moments, she had been. Under the golden glow of the chandeliers, with the swirling sounds of the orchestra in the background, he'd gazed at her as though she were some priceless treasure. In his eyes, she'd read forever. And she'd felt like her heart was just going to explode with emotion.

All her imagination, though, because when the song ended, so had the look, and she'd barely seen him the rest of the night.

Her mother elbowed her. "Kneel," she hissed.

Obediently, Keely sank down onto the crimson velvet cushion.

It had turned strange. She wasn't quite sure why or how, but something was off. Maybe something had happened, maybe too much of what she felt had shown in her eyes. Whatever it was, Lex was already backing away.

And she hadn't a clue what to do.

Lex unlocked the front door quietly. The last thing he was in the mood for was company. If it had been a different time of year, he'd have just kept walking but after an hour of sub-freezing temperatures, it was too cold to stay outside.

Even for him.

So he opened the door as stealthily as he could manage, trying not to think that it was damned silly for a grown man to sneak in like a guilty high schooler come back from being out all night. He was too old to be tiptoeing down halls. One more example of how out off-kilter his life had become.

Which he really needed to deal with at some point. He needed to have a quiet, diplomatic sit down with Olivia and get this worked out. No, what he *needed* was to solve the Bradley problem so that he could leave.

"Well, you're up early," Olivia said from the breakfast nook, startling him.

"So are you," he responded, then took a conscious breath. It wasn't her fault he was in a hell of a mood that morning.

"I went to early Mass," she said, fingering her pearls. "I knocked to see if you wanted to come but you were out."

"I went for a walk." He made himself sit and took coffee from the maid. "Why didn't you sleep in and go to a later service? I figured you'd want to take it easy on your first gala-free day. Rest on your laurels. You did a great job."

"It did come off well, didn't it? Our biggest yet, the ticket committee told me."

"Everyone looked like they were having a good time."

"Except you." At his guilty start, the corners of her

mouth curved slightly. "You did a good job of pretend-ing, but I could tell you were miserable most of the time. And I could also tell when you weren't." She paused. "I saw you dancing with Keely Stafford."

Lex let out a long, slow breath. "I danced with a lot of people. I danced with you."

"And you danced with her."

"Why shouldn't I? We're all kind of in this together, aren't we? I like her." And he was very afraid that like had turned into something more, something that was going to be dangerous if he didn't watch it.

"Just don't get too caught up in her. She was your brother's fiancée, don't forget."

Lex felt his jaw tighten. "I'm aware of that. I also don't think that matters much, given the present situa-tion."

"I wasn't the only one who noticed, you know. And commented."

"Let me guess," he said. "Alicia Smythe."

"Joyce Barron, actually."

Equally as loathsome, as far as he was concerned. "She can mind her own business. Not that it matters what she thinks."

"It matters to me," Olivia said tartly. "Keely Stafford was involved with your brother, got him to propose to her and then all this trouble broke out. I won't have you paying that kind of attention to her. It makes us all look ridiculous."

Lex stared at her. "Ridiculous? Do you hear your-self? Are you completely forgetting the fact that Bradley was the one who got you both into this mess? Keely's doing everything she possibly can to get you off the hook. I'd focus more on that and stop listening to trash-talking witches."

"Those 'trash-talking witches,' as you call them, happen to be my friends."

"Are you so sure about that? I'd say your friend is the person I'm working with to clear your name."

Olivia's gaze cooled. "Are you doing anything else with her?"

Yes, he was—but what, exactly? "I spend ninety-five percent of my time in places like the Sudan and Lebanon," he said shortly. "You want to tell me how I'm supposed to get involved with anyone?"

"That's not an answer to my question."

"It's the only one you're going to get." Courtesy, he believed in. Pointless accountability, he didn't. "Mom, I turned thirty last summer. A medical miracle, I realize, since you're only twenty-nine yourself, but still…"

"I don't want you involved with her." She folded her arms.

He looked at her, staring at him defiantly like some Victorian matron. Whatever world she thought gave her that kind of authority, he didn't belong in it. He met her eyes with a look equally as resolved. A humming silence stretched out between them.

Olivia cracked first. "I don't want to fight with you," she said.

"That's good. I don't want to fight with you, either."

"There's just a lot going on. Bill Hartley is pressuring me. We have to make a decision on the new director this week."

"So what's holding you up?"

"They want my recommendations."

"The answer," he said, "is still no."

"You don't know the question yet."

The hell he didn't. "Did you forget what I just said about ninety-five percent of my time? That's where I belong. Not here, not on the board. For the last time, find someone else." The room suddenly felt stifling. Lex rose. "I'm going to get out of here and check e-mail."

He headed out to the hall, Olivia hot on his heels. "But we can't have someone else. We need you."

"No, you don't."

He entered Pierce's office and headed for the desk. Olivia slipped past him and stood in his way. "Aubrey Pierce Alexander, you stop right there and listen to me." Despite himself, Lex stopped short. "That company is our family legacy. It's only right that control stays in our hands, in the person of a family member who can carry on the Alexander line of succession. And that means you."

It was as if he could hear the shackles clamped around his ankles. "No, Mom. *No.* It doesn't mean me."

"Then who else do you suggest?" she snapped. "I need someone who's looking out for this family's interests. This is your legacy, Trey, whether you want it to be or not. It's in your blood. It's your future."

"No," he blazed. "It's not my future. Why the hell do you think I left? Why do you think I've stayed away all these years?"

"You left because you were angry at your father," she retorted. "Let it go. He's gone. He had flaws but he's gone, and all staying angry with him is going to do is hurt you, the family and the family's future."

Fury boiled up in him. "*I'm* hurting the family's

future? I am? You've got one Alexander who couldn't tell his home life from his business life and the other who's in hiding because he flushed some criminal's money through the corporate accounts. That's the family legacy I'm supposed to uphold?" He leaned down toward her, his face only inches from hers. "I want my own life, not version three of the Aubrey Pierce Alexander corporate dynasty. I am not Pierce—thank God—and I sure as hell am not Bradley. You want someone in the family to be on the board, then dammit, do it yourself."

Anger seethed in the room like some kind of a living thing. Each click of the clock sounded like a mallet being struck.

"I see." Olivia's voice was as brittle as glass. "Well. Excuse me. I won't take up any more of your time."

A nice quiet, diplomatic conversation. Perfect.

"Mom, wait," Lex said, but she'd already gone.

He stared at the photographs on the walls: Pierce, his parents together. Bradley and Pierce side by side on the family sailboat, the one Bradley had inherited, destined now to be confiscated and auctioned off to the highest bidder.

On the day captured in the photo, though, that was all off in the unimaginable future. Bradley and Pierce leaned shoulder to shoulder, holding a race trophy they'd just won, putting on toothy smiles for the camera. The day Bradley had inherited the *All In* had no doubt been his proudest moment.

People usually use the name of someone or something important. Lex stiffened. The boat, he thought. It had to be the boat.

And he rose.

* * *

Keely and her parents walked out of the church, squinting in the late-morning sunlight. The bells of the carillon sounded in the background.

"Lovely sermon, Reverend," Jeannie said warmly, shaking his hand.

"Glad you enjoyed it. And it's been a pleasure to have *you* back." He smiled at Keely with eyes so twinkly she wondered if he knew just how long it had been since she'd been to services.

A snatch of My Chemical Romance shattered the silence. Blushing furiously, Keely dug out her phone.

"Excuse me," Keely muttered, and hurried down the steps. "Hello?"

"Keely? Lex," he said briefly. "Where are you? Can you get loose?"

"I'm just coming out of church. What's up?"

"I just figured out something that might be our answer."

"To what?"

"The password. What church are you at?"

"St. Stephen's, over on Hollis."

"Great. I'll be by in ten minutes."

It was closer to five when his Jeep swung up.

"I've got to go," Keely told Jeannie, and kissed her goodbye.

She couldn't help noticing the stares as she walked to the vehicle. So much for staying under the radar, she thought in resignation.

"You found the password?" she asked as she shut the door and snapped on her seatbelt.

"Not exactly. But I think I have a good guess. If I'm right, this might all be over."

The snow they'd had since the last time they were up at the house had done the road no good. The Jeep bounced over the ruts with a tooth-rattling vigor that made it impossible to talk.

Little else had changed since their last visit, she saw when they arrived. The new snow lay in a pristine white layer over the yard and the steps, broken only by the small tracks of some little rodent.

"So are you ever going to tell me about this flash of inspiration you had?" Keely asked as Lex swung open the door.

"The boat. Bradley's boat."

"The *All In?*"

"Exactly." He strode ahead of her through the living room and down the hall. She did her best to ignore the door at the end that led to the master bedroom. Lex didn't seem to notice.

"People use things that are important to them for passwords, right? Bradley was crazy for sailing from the time he was a kid. There was the picture of you guys on the boat and there's a picture of him and my father on it hanging in Pierce's office." He pulled out the laptop case. "So I figured the best thing to do was get over here and try it. If I'm right, all our problems are solved."

All their problems were solved?

Not even close, she thought.

Keely opened the laptop and hit the power button. The machine came on with a hum. "It was nice dancing with you at the gala last night," she said, wondering if he'd even noticed that they hadn't kissed hello or touched once since he'd picked her up. There was a weird sort of frenetic energy to him. After all the times she'd felt so connected, she suddenly felt like there was no communication there at all.

The log-in screen came up. Lex leaned over her, bracing his hands on the desk beside her. Their faces were very nearly side by side as she tabbed down to the password line and keyed in *all in*.

"Come on, baby," he murmured to the computer, his fingers pressing into the desktop.

Keely pressed Enter.

And the log-in screen disappeared.

"Yes!" Lex crowed, arms up.

The background screen appeared, a photograph of a tropical beach, complete with pale blue water and palm trees.

"Looks nice on a thirty degree day, doesn't it?" Keely sighed.

"You find the files we need on this computer and I'll send you there," Lex said, oblivious to the quick glance she shot him.

With a few clicks of the keys, she brought up the file tree. "Better yet, we could go together," she said, keeping her tone as light as his. "A reward for hard work. Bradley and I were going to Barbados for our honeymoon. I still have the tickets for the package."

Lex was back to leaning over her shoulder. "I thought the guy bought those."

She shrugged. "Bradley wasn't big on organizing. I was sort of the one who took care of it all so everything's in my name. Fully paid for and transferable." She hesitated. "Maybe we could take a getaway when this is all over."

She held her breath for his response but all he said was, "Let's hope that's soon," and stared at the screen.

Files were there, that much was certain. The problem was, they only documented the operation. They didn't do anything to clear her or Olivia. Not that she and Lex didn't look and look hard. Keely opened spreadsheets, she opened PDFs. She opened text document after text document, even image files. She discovered the full world of Bradley's secret universe, even a fake identity.

But she didn't find the one piece of information she sought.

"We're missing something," Lex said, pacing around the room. "He's got all kinds of documentation but nothing to really incriminate Skele. Why go to all this trouble and not keep leverage?"

"Maybe it's in his e-mail." Keely opened the e-mail application. "I can't really imagine anyone putting anything incriminating in e-mail but we might get lucky."

The software finished loading and the launch page appeared.

Bradley was scrupulously neat when it came to his e-mail. He didn't have the usual tangle of messages in his Inbox or Sent Items. He'd structured a slew of folders, each empty, each with a cryptic name.

Save for one.

"Interesting," Keely murmured.

"What?" Lex asked, watching her closely.

"He's got a VoIP line."

"Voype?" Lex echoed.

She smiled. "V-O-I-P. It stands for voice over Internet protocol."

"Pretend I'm someone who spends the bulk of his time in Third World countries and war zones," Lex said.

Keely felt the pang. She didn't have to pretend. She swallowed. "VoIP is telephone service over the Internet. You can skip phone lines altogether, most of the time—the Internet carries the calls. The service can be spotty but it's incredibly cheap. I have it at my apartment." She switched to the web browser. "As long as you've got a telephone and their little widget, you can make and receive phone calls from anywhere you can hook up your computer."

"Without changing the number?"

She nodded. "You could call me at my 212 Manhattan number and I could actually be in Tuscaloosa. And I could call you from there and you would still see me as calling from the 212 area code."

Lex flicked her a quick glance. "He couldn't be traced."

"Not easily, especially if he was using cable modem to get the VoIP service. The account's under his false identity, so it's not traceable to him, or even to this house."

"Sweet."

"There's another nice little aspect to it all. You can check your voice mail online, as well as by phone."

"By text or by sound?"

"It plays it on your computer. If we can get into his account at the VoIP Web site, we can not only see a detailed log of every incoming and outgoing call, we can get audio files of every message."

She was grasping at straws, she knew, but she was damned if she was going to give up. When the VoIP site loaded, she crossed her fingers and clicked on the fill button on the browser to see if it would complete the username and password for her.

The lines stayed resolutely blank. Unsurprised, she entered Bradley's e-mail address and *all in* for the password.

Username or password incorrect, the screen said.

At least this time around they didn't have to run in circles to get the password. She clicked on the "Forgot your password?" link. Confidently, she entered the first initial and last name of Bradley's false identity, along with the e-mail address and clicked Submit.

Error: Username or e-mail address incorrect.

This, she hadn't expected. The password was supposed to be the hard part. "Trust Bradley to make it difficult," she said, typing first name, last initial.

Error: Username or e-mail address incorrect. Over the next fifteen minutes, she tried his real name, his parents' names, the boat, the company, every combination and permutation she could think of. Always with the same result.

Error: Username or e-mail address incorrect.

If she saw it one more time, she was going to scream.

"Dammit." Lex slapped his hand on the desktop and began to pace again, practically vibrating with frustration. "I thought we were home free. We'd get you and Mom off the hook, we could get the laptop to Stockton so he can nail his case and we could all finally get back to our lives."

We could all finally get back to our lives.

And there it was, out in the open.

"Is that what happens?" Keely asked quietly. "We stay out of jail and you fly away?"

Lex turned to her. "When I get another assignment."

She knew it, she knew that was the unspoken agreement and yet something in her had to try. Something in her couldn't give up.

Lex let out a slow breath. "Keely, look, you know I came here to clear my mother's name."

"And I guess I was just entertainment along the way." Her voice sounded far away to her own ears.

"No." He looked at her steadily. "You weren't. You're not. But…I can't stay here. I just can't. And I don't know where I'm going to end up next—or how long I'll be there."

"So you just ride on the wind." Unable to sit still, she rose and went to the window. "And I guess if I start to feel anything for you, that's just my problem."

"I'm not trying to hurt you."

"But you're sure as hell doing a good job, aren't you?" She turned back to him, eyes bright.

"I just don't see how it makes sense for us to try to keep this going when I'm going to be all over the place, probably for months at a time."

"There's a way if you want to. You could do something crazy like stay."

Lex closed his eyes and shook his head. "No, I can't. Believe me, I can't."

"You can't or you don't want to? It really comes

down to the same thing, doesn't it?" And it was killing her, killing her. "So I guess we stick with the program, then—we find the files, Olivia and I get to stay out of jail, thanks to your heroic efforts and you get to ride off into the sunset. Except that part's ahead of schedule, isn't it?" Her voice sharpened. "You're already gone."

"What's that supposed to mean?"

"Last night at the gala, when we were dancing. I saw it in your face. You were there and then mentally you were just…gone. Like you went away in your head. Like today. We haven't even brushed hands, we haven't even touched."

Temper flickered in his eyes. "I'm sorry, I thought we were focusing on keeping your butt out of jail."

"Sure, because then you can go."

"And why the hell not?" he snapped. "I had a nice happy career before all this happened, Keely. A life and an interesting job that kept me thousands of miles away from here, which is just where I wanted to be. That's me—that's the way I am. You want a guy who's going to stick around? What you're looking for isn't me. I can't step into Bradley's shoes."

"I don't want you to be Bradley," she said furiously.

"Sure you do." He stalked across the room. "Everybody does. My mom wants someone to sit on the Alexander board, manage her finances, escort her to events, be her company at breakfast. You want that sturdy, dependable lover, a guy you can substitute on your honeymoon trip. Settle in and maybe rearrange some flowers when we get back. Sorry, I can't do this."

"*I* want a lover?" she repeated incredulously. "You were the one who pushed this, you were the one who made it happen. What happened Lex, did you scare yourself?" she demanded. "Is this all too real for you? Oh, I forgot, you're the guy without connections, the one who walked away from his family, his home."

"Dammit, I'm sick to death of everyone trying to tell me about where my home is and what I owe to my family," he exploded. "Everybody's grabbing at me to stay—you, my mother, Darlene, Flaherty. I'm not some domesticated animal you can strap to a water-wheel and lead around in circles. I'm not my father, I'm not Bradley. I can't replace him or put a ring on your finger and make it all better, or be the guy that he wasn't."

"I'm not looking for a replacement for Bradley," she said hotly. "I didn't love Bradley. I love you."

He turned from her, closed his eyes. "Oh, God, Keely, don't do that. It just makes it worse."

Keely felt the blood drain from her face. And that quickly, the anger dissipated into a frozen mist. "It's not your choice," she said, strangely calm. "You can't keep people from caring for you, Lex. You can tell yourself that you cruise through life without connections all you want. You're lying to yourself. And you're lying to yourself if you try to say it makes you happy. Now, where's that iPod you said you saw?"

She went to rummage for it on the coffee table, knowing she had to concentrate on finding the familiar blue player, on something, or go mad.

"Keely?"

She looked up and saw Lex holding out the player. "We have to—"

"Thank you." She cut him off and pushed gently past him, heading for the door. "Now, I think we've done all we can do here. I'd appreciate it if you'd take me home."

Chapter Thirteen

She didn't cry. Instead, she was eerily calm. She might have felt absolutely frozen inside but she didn't cry. Not while they packed away the computer, not during the silent drive home. Not even when he pulled up before her parents' house and turned to her.

"So what happens now?"

Keely studied the glove-compartment latch. "We're running out of things to check and time's running out on us. Let's give it until after Christmas. If we haven't found the password by then, we turn the laptop over to Stockton and let him take it from there."

"What if they don't find anything to exonerate you?"

She gave a humorless smile. "Then we hire good lawyers. That's one place connections come in handy."

He winced. "Keely—"

"No." She opened the door. "I think we've talked enough for one day, Lex. Let's just leave it at that."

"But I—"

"No." And she got out.

She might have sworn she could hear the shattering of her heart as she walked away, but her eyes were dry, and her eyes were dry when she walked into the house to find her mother at the dining table.

"How did everything go?" Jeannie asked.

Keely's throat tightened. How could she possibly answer that? "It was a bust. We didn't find what we were hoping for." She'd hoped for love and instead she'd found a man whose life was built around avoiding it. She'd fallen for two Alexander brothers. One, the good brother, had proven to be bad through and through. The other, the bad brother, had turned out to be good.

And she had lost them both, one by walking away, the other by wanting him to stay.

"I think I'm going to take a swim," Keely said quickly but something had gone funny with her voice.

Jeannie rose slowly from the table and put a hand to Keely's cheek. "What's wrong?" she asked.

"Everything," Keely said.

And then, finally, she did cry.

The darkroom had always been his place. Even during the crazy times growing up, it had been a sanctuary. There, among the safe light and the tongs and trays, he could warp time and space. He could walk in and hours could bleed away while he played with different exposures and papers, with dodging and burning, until the image in his mind emerged. It was his own form of meditation. No matter what was bothering him, when he stepped into the darkroom, it went away. Things might have gone to hell with Keely, he might be getting covered in icicles every time he walked near Olivia, but the darkroom would make it all okay.

Except that this time around, it wasn't working. Lex stood in the rental darkroom trying to think about how he wanted the prints to look and all he could see was Keely, that soft, vulnerable mouth and that gut-shot look on her face at the end. Because it was the end, he knew it.

He'd wanted, God, he'd wanted more than anything to wipe that look away. Unfortunately, the one thing that would do it was impossible. There was no point in asking why she couldn't understand because there was no way she could unless she was standing in his shoes. It was ridiculous to think about trying to keep something going between them. It wasn't fair to her. That was the only reason.

Not because it scared the hell out of him.

He glanced down at the tray of developer in his hand and cursed as he saw the blotches on the prints. Once again, he'd gotten distracted. He'd been at it for over an hour without getting a single print that was usable by his standards. He just couldn't make it work.

Like things with him and Keely.

His cell phone rang and he flipped it open, happy for an excuse to stop.

"Alexander."

"And what are you up to this fine day, me bhoyo," asked Flaherty.

"Developing prints. You remember me, Flaherty, the photographer?"

"Ah, that I do. Though barely. It's been a week since I talked to you."

"'Zat right?" Lex aligned a sheet of linen paper on the enlarger.

"Did it ever occur to you to call me?"

"You said take some time and think about it. I'm thinking."

"For a week?"

With one hand, he pressed the button that exposed the paper. "I'm a virtuoso thinker. Take's time to do these things right."

"I'll say. So what did you decide?"

"Did I say I'd made a decision?" He slid the print into the bath of developer and checked his watch.

Flaherty snorted. "If I know you, you made a decision within fifteen minutes of me telling you about it."

Actually, for about the first time in his life, Lex hadn't. Habit screamed for him to turn the spot down but he couldn't quite do it. How was it that after so miserably bollixing things up with Keely in the name of his freedom, the idea of spending a year stateside could suddenly be so appealing?

"Tell you what, Flaherty." He sloshed the developer around. "I'll come into town next week and we can talk about it some more, start getting more specific."

"Does that mean yes?" Flaherty asked eagerly.

"Not yet," Lex said, "but it's a start."

Keely stroked down the length of the pool, feeling the water move over her body. She swam a lot these days; something about the activity and the soothing flow of the water made her feel less like screaming. And it was the one place she could weep without anyone asking questions.

Her parents did their best to be sympathetic without hovering. Lydia's brand of sympathy ran more to ropes and gelding with dull knives, but in the interest of wearing her New Year's dress versus being in prison, she'd agreed not to do anything drastic. But Keely didn't have a place of her own to curl up in misery. Oh, she could go to her apartment, but all she'd face there would be memories of Lex. Anyway, it was best not to give into it any more than she had to. She was still working at the shop. She needed to keep things on an even keel.

And hide the fact that her heart was broken to pieces.

It was a funny thing about heartbreak. When you were shattered inside, it was hard to care about much of anything. The issues that had troubled her for weeks somehow seemed minor. She couldn't muster up the emotional energy to worry about Bradley or Stockton or any of the trouble at her doorstep. The only thing that mattered was the loss and emptiness that made the days endless.

And so she swam. She swam and she wept and she waited for the days to go by. Eventually, Lex would leave again. Time would pass and maybe there would come a day when he wasn't the first thought on her mind in the morning and the last thought at night. Maybe someday she would get over him.

But she didn't see it happening for a very long time.

* * *

Lex walked into the house. Christmas was just days away. It was a time for houses to be jumping with life and joy, not silence. Olivia hadn't even bothered to put up a tree, he realized suddenly. The decorations were up, but no pine stood in its traditional spot next to the mantel.

There was something a little melancholy about that.

"Lex?" It was Olivia's voice. He turned to see her at the entrance to the room.

They'd barely talked since their altercation the previous Sunday. The few times he'd tried to initiate a conversation, Olivia had frozen him out. It was easier just to flee to the bakery or the darkroom.

Or the safe house, where he sat on the steps and stared out into the woods.

"What do you need, Mom?"

Was it his imagination or did she wince a bit at the question?

"Can we talk a minute?" She nodded to one of the couches. After a pause, he sat. Olivia let out a breath. "I need to apologize."

"No more than I do. I flew off the handle Sunday. I shouldn't have."

She shook her head. "You had every reason."

"I'm supposed to be here to help, not kick you when you're down."

"I'm an adult. I should start learning how to help myself." She studied her hands. "It's not easy to admit but you were right. I spent my life letting Pierce take care of things, then when he was gone, Bradley."

"It was a bad time."

"I let it go on too long. Deep down I knew better but it was so much easier to let Bradley handle it all. And it was a comfort, having him around. Life didn't seem so…empty." She glanced around. "It's a big house. Too big for one. I didn't want to sell it because it's the family home and because, well, I always hoped you or Bradley might want it. But your life isn't here. I realize that now. And wishing won't make it so."

"Mom," he said helplessly.

"Don't." She squared her shoulders in that motion he'd seen so many times. "I need to take charge of my own affairs."

"You can," he assured her. "You will. If you can pull off that gala, you can do anything you want to do."

"You think so?"

"Yeah."

A hint of a smile glimmered then in her eyes. "You know, I think I'm going to test that theory out. I've called Bill Hartley." She paused. "I'm taking that seat on the board."

"You what?"

"I'm taking that seat on the board."

"Attagirl." With a whoop, Lex grabbed her up and spun her around. "I'll give you three years before you're running the place."

"Two and a half," she corrected with a smile. It was a shaky one but it was a start.

Lex grinned down at her and then he had an idea. "So do you have any place to be right now?" he asked.

Olivia frowned. "No. Why?"

He put his hands in his pockets and rocked back on his heels. "I noticed this room is missing a little something. How about if you and I go out and buy ourselves a Christmas tree?"

"Have I ever told you how much I love you?" she asked, wrapping her arms around him.

And the smile was back full force.

"Okay, the forms are all in this folder, ready to be signed." Keely pointed down to the IRS forms, neatly clipped to envelopes, sitting on Darlene's desk. "You send them in and be sure you do your electronic deposit and you should be all set."

"That's great," Darlene said, scribbling her name at the bottoms. She glanced up. "Where's the invoice? What do I owe you?"

"A cruller." Keely laughed. "You don't owe me a thing. I'm happy to do it."

"I'm happy that you're happy, but I'm in business and so are you. If you do work, then you charge me."

"I'm not in business."

"Why not?" Darlene asked. "We need another accountant here. George left a lot of people high and dry when he moved. Tanya at the salon and Lenny at the DVD rental place, Andover Hardware, they've all been complaining. If I put the word around, I could get you a dozen clients right away."

"Oh, I don't know," Keely hedged. "It's been nice being here but I've got an apartment and a job in Manhattan. It's a big leap to—" She stopped.

"What?"

Was that what it felt like to Lex, this sudden sense of being hustled into a big decision that she might not be ready for?

"It's just a big change," she finished lamely. "Manhattan's where my job and home are."

"But what about your heart?" Darlene watched her closely.

With a pair of green eyes and a quick laugh. With a man who didn't want her love. Keely swallowed. "Crullers," she said brightly. "My heart's with crullers."

If he was going to play Santa, Christmas Eve was as good a time as any to do it. Especially when he was stir-crazy. Lex skipped the red suit and white beard and just stuck with his jeans and black jacket. He figured the sticky snow that had been coming down all evening would do the rest.

He stood on the front doorstep, feeling a little uneasy as he knocked. After all, she didn't know he was coming. He wasn't even sure she'd want him to be there. Maybe she wouldn't be home. Maybe he'd be better off just setting the box on the doorstep and going.

But just as he was turning away, the door opened.

He swallowed. "Merry Christmas."

"Merry Christmas!" Darlene beamed. "Come in, come in. What a surprise."

He'd never been to her home before. It was small and cozy, with the same warm clutter as the bakery, with one exception. Actually, several exceptions.

Lex frowned. "Just how many cats do you have?" he asked.

"Seven," Darlene said with a fond smile. "And one husband. Dick, look who's here."

Dick, almost as wide as Darlene, was a computer programmer. Lex wasn't sure he'd ever heard the man utter more than a single sentence at a time. "Merry Christmas," Dick mumbled, and immediately got up and left the room.

"I didn't mean to drive him away."

"Oh, don't worry about him. He's got a regular Monday-night online chat with his Linux-developers group. So what did you bring me?" She looked bright-eyed at his package with its poor excuse of a wrapping job.

"Just a little something I thought you might get a kick out of."

She tore in with enthusiasm, popping the ribbon and ripping away the paper and the padding to reveal his gift. And stared.

It was a photo of the bakery, taken from the street so that you could see the display window with its pyramids of meringues and croissant and cupcakes. Townspeople gossiped at the tables and in the back, Darlene held court at the counter, putting a cruller in a bag, her mouth curved with a smile so wide you could hear the laughter.

"Oh, Lex," she breathed, blinking quickly.

"I printed it on linen paper so that it has the sepia look. You'll maybe want a different frame but I thought you could put it up in the bakery somewhere."

"I love it." She gave him a fierce hug and turned back to the picture. "And everybody's in it. Look, Reverend Richards and Tanya and Harry Lonnroth and—"

And Keely. Shining blond hair, laughing eyes, mischief in the very set of her shoulders as she reached for the bag of crullers. He'd seen her in the picture as soon as he looked at the negatives. At first, he'd been tempted to choose another shot but this was the one that most truly captured Darlene and the bakery. And in the end, it was the one he went with.

"Takes a pretty photograph, doesn't she?" Darlene asked. "At least she used to. I don't know how they'd come out today. She's kind of got that walking-zombie look these days." She glanced up at him. "Kind of like you. Want to tell me what's going on?"

He shook his head. "Nothing's going on. We're just not having any luck finding the proof we need."

"Not a good thing. Then again, I suppose if you find it, you're just going to be off, so maybe that's not such a good thing, either."

"We had this conversation last Sunday," he said.

"And I seem to recall telling you it was kind of nice having you around. Back when you and Keely were walking around looking ready to tap-dance on the moon."

"Sticking around isn't what I do," he said.

Or was it? Connections. They'd formed all around him when he hadn't been paying attention. His mother, Flaherty, Darlene. Keely. They weren't supposed to matter to him. He was supposed to be able to go and not look back, go and not worry about anyone else.

But why had he sent a postcard to Darlene from every place he'd gone? *You can tell yourself that you cruise through life without connections all you want. You're lying to yourself.* He heard Keely's voice. And he remembered the shadows in her eyes as she'd walked away.

"Freedom can be its own kind of trap," Darlene said gently.

And he stared down at the laughing Keely in the photo

and wondered what the hell he was doing. "Maybe," he said slowly, and rose. "But it's what I know."

Darlene shook her head. "Why won't you—" Her sentence ended in a squeak as the room went dark. "Dick!" she yelled. "Did you throw the breaker again?"

There was some thumping and bumping and then Dick appeared, flashlight in hand. "No, I wasn't doing anything. I think the power's out, look." He went to the window where the streetlights were dark. "I was just down in a chat room and boom, the room was dark except for my laptop screen. Power's up somewhere, though. The town WiFi's still going."

Olivia, thought Lex. "I'd better get going," he said, with a sneaky relief. "My mom's at home alone and I want to make sure she's okay."

"Well, be careful. The roads are already messy enough without live power lines in the street. Get home safely, that's what's important." She leaned in to kiss his cheek. "Thank you for my gift."

"My pleasure. Merry Christmas," he said.

The scent of pine, a crackling fire, gifts under the tree, Nat King Cole on the stereo singing Christmas carols. It should have been a perfect Christmas Eve, a magical one with snowflakes drifting down outside the window.

To Keely, it simply meant that she'd almost made it through another day.

She sat curled in an armchair, trying to read, but the conversation with Darlene kept coming back to her. Staying in Chilton. Starting her own business. Two days before when Darlene had first suggested it, it had seemed ludicrous. A year ago, a month ago, even, it would have been unthinkable. Now?

Now it was what she wanted, she realized abruptly. Oh, not staying in her parents' house, not working full time at the flower shop, but if she were to get her own place, start her own business? She could build a life she could love.

And as she opened her mouth to tell them, the lights went out.

The silence was complete, the tree was dark. The light from the fire kept the room from being completely black. After the first heart-stopping instants, Keely's eyes began to adjust so that she could see the windows.

"I'll get the flashlight," Carter said, standing up after it was clear that the power wasn't coming back anytime soon.

Jeannie moved over to the mantel to light the candles that stood there. "Decorative, as well as functional," she said.

"And these are ugly but functional," Carter said, walking in with a trio of giant flashlights. "Everybody gets one."

The novelty of the power outage faded quickly. With the music and twinkling lights gone, the festivity bled away and the shadows gathered around her, the emotional ones.

To hold them at bay, she rose and went back to the guest room for her iPod. There had to be something, some way for her to keep it together. Dance music, something with a beat.

She sank back into the armchair. Ok Go, she

decided, fast, catchy and clever. When she tried to roll down the menu to the album title, though, she slipped past it.

"You know, just once you'd think I could work this thing right," she said.

"What, dear?" Jeannie asked.

"My iPod."

"I'm going to have a drink, assuming I can find the bar in the dark," her father said. "Either of you want one?"

"A Bailey's, please," Jeannie said.

"Keely?"

Glancing up, she passed the name of the band again. "Um, sure. That would be good." Shaking her head, she rolled back up the menu, paying attention and taking care to get it right.

The Ok Go weren't on it.

Frowning, she ran up the menu. Nope, definitely not there. And as she looked, she realized that they weren't the only ones. There was another band missing, and another and another. And another. It was an iPod she had in her hand, all right.

It just wasn't hers.

Bradley's she assumed, it had to be Bradley's. So maybe he'd gotten one on his own and just hadn't told her. He always had liked blue. And if he'd planned from the beginning to leave it at the safe house, it didn't matter if the two looked alike.

Still, there had to be something on the player that she could stand listening to. Forget artists, she'd just go to search by genre so that she could avoid the one labeled insipid Top 40 pop.

One of the ways she and Bradley were different—

the many ways, she now knew—was in music. She preferred quirky and alternative, he went for Ashlee Simpson and Britney Spears. Of course, maybe he'd liked the singers better than the music. That should have tipped her off right there.

Interesting that the betrayal no longer had the power to hurt her. The ache she felt for Lex left no room for it.

It took only that to remind her, only that to bring it back. And tonight, of all nights, there were no distractions. No power, no games to play, no movies or television to watch. Just music, a book by flashlight and the slow, measured tick of the clock as the time crawled by.

She just missed him. She missed the person she could talk with, who understood what she meant without her having to explain it, the man who could make her laugh helplessly and who could moments later have her crying out in ecstasy. It didn't matter that he couldn't be there for her, it didn't matter that his life was elsewhere, she wanted him, just wanted him. For an instant, the memory of being in his arms was so vivid that loss took her breath away.

She closed her eyes and rested her forehead on her hand and fought back the grief. He was doing something different, he was going somewhere else. They weren't right for each other, pure and simple. However much she felt down to her DNA that they belonged together, it wasn't going to work and she had to accept that and move on.

"You okay?"

She glanced up to see a highball glass with her

family's traditional Christmas drink and dredged up a smile. "Thanks, Dad."

"My pleasure, pumpkin." He leaned down and kissed her on the forehead.

She went back to the iPod and blinked when the wrong menu came up. She'd clicked on the wrong line again, she realized, choosing Extras rather than Genres. She moved to jump up the menu tree but stopped. On the list under Extras was an entry called Notes. Curious, she clicked on it and saw a handful of entries: BRD MTG, TREE, PW, VPW.

PW.

Password? Heart thumping a little faster, Keely clicked on that filename and the entry came up, two lines.

User: BAlexander
Pass: All In

The hair prickled on the back of her neck as she ran back up a level. VPW.

VoIP password, it had to be.

She was up off the chair before she even thought about it, heart pounding.

"Keely, where are you going?" her mother said, startled.

"To use the comp—" She stopped. The power was out. That meant neither of her parents' computers would work. She needed a laptop. Now. She wasn't going to wait, she wasn't about to wait, not with the key possibly here in her hands.

After all, what else did she have to do?

"Can I use the car?" she asked breathlessly.

"Where are you going at this hour? The power's out over half of town."

"I'll take a flashlight. There's something I have to check," she said in a rush. "I'll be back."

Chapter Fourteen

Olivia sat at the desk in Pierce's office. A Mozart concerto played over the sound system, a cup of tea sat at her elbow. Calming. The backup generators had kicked on a few seconds after the power had gone out. The house was dimmer than usual, though. With Lex out and Corinne gone for the holiday, it felt cavernous and empty.

And it made her uneasy. Having the doorbell ring a few minutes after the lights went out shouldn't have made her jump like it did, though. She'd merely been surprised; she'd been even more surprised when she'd opened the door to discover Keely Stafford waiting there. And she as was nice as could be. Lex would have been proud of how nicely she let Keely in to go through God only knew what in Pierce's office.

Olivia certainly wasn't about to ask. She was still smarting from Lex's chiding the previous week. It wasn't easy to have your child go toe to toe with you.

It was even less easy when that child was right.

She tried to concentrate on the copy of the Alexander Technologies Annual Report that sat before her. If she was going to do this, she was going to do it right, and that meant following the company all the way back to when Pierce first took over.

From the hallway came the sound of the front door opening. Olivia stood with relief. She was serious about her new venture but she was human. It was Christmas Eve and she would far and away rather be relaxing with her son.

"Trey, I'm in here. Did you run into traff—"

She stopped dead. Relaxing with her son. It was her son who stood before her, but not Trey. It was Bradley, looking puffy faced and pale. Next to him, stocky and stolid, stood a man she didn't recognize.

"Bradley," she whispered, and stepped forward to envelope him in a hug. He moved away from her a little bit, though, so that she just stood before him, staring in confusion. "You're back. We've been so worried."

"Everything's fine," he said. "Merry Christmas."

"Merry Christmas," she said faintly, staring at him. "This is—"

"No introductions," the man ordered, a whisper of foreign lands in his words. He had the implacable face of a bully, someone comfortable using force and size to intimidate.

"I can't stay long. I'm sure you understand," Bradley said to her.

"What have you done? They've been saying things about you, terrible things. Did you really take all of that money? Why did you run away?"

"Lot of questions, Mom." A faint smile curved his lips and suddenly she knew.

It was all true.

"Turn yourself in," she said urgently. "We can get you good lawyers, the best—"

"You've got to know I can't do that." He put his arm around her shoulders and steered her into the living room. "Now, you go sit—"

"She comes with us," the man interrupted.

Bradley's head snapped around toward him. "All right."

It made her skin crawl to walk down to the office with them, to wait in the doorway trying to stand as far as possible from the stolid man. While Bradley went inside. And then she heard Bradley curse.

"Where is it?" he demanded, looking up from where he'd spilled out the contents of the bowl all over the desk.

"What?" Olivia asked.

"You know what. The key."

She blinked. "I don't know what you're talking about."

"Who's been here?"

"Bradley, it doesn't matter. You need to turn yourself in. You need to let us help you."

"Then help me," he snapped. "Who's been in here?"

"Trey," she said helplessly. "Keely. Corinne, to clean. But—"

"We need no key," said the companion. "We go."

"Can you pick—"

"We go," he said again.

Bradley nodded sharply and strode out of the office.

"Where are you going?" she said, hurrying after them. "This isn't going to help you. You've got to give yourself up. We can get a team of good lawyers, make a deal."

He turned to her at the door. "I can't make a deal, Mom. It's too late."

"But—"

"I've got to go." He kissed her forehead. "Merry Christmas."

She'd done smarter things than carting off to the safe house on her own, Keely acknowledged, peering out at the rising road. In daylight, with a four-wheel drive, the road had been challenge enough. At night, with fresh snow, the sedan she'd borrowed from her parents barely managed to get up the slope. Why hadn't she waited for Lex?

Because she didn't think she could bear to see him again.

She'd crossed her fingers as she'd driven up to Olivia's house, and breathed a sigh of relief when she'd found him gone. It was the work of a minute to grab the key. With luck, she'd be in, find the files, and get out without running into him. She could send the data to Stockton, solve her and Olivia's problems and go on with her life.

It all sounded so tidy when she thought of it that way.

Too bad it wasn't.

Her windshield wipers slapped back and forth, rubbing away the fresh flakes of snow. At the edges of her windshield, a little layer of slush had begun accumulating. A white Christmas, she thought. It had always portended good things.

But that had been before.

Lex walked through the door to the house, his mood scarcely any better. The roads had been worse than Darlene's predictions. Downed power lines had blocked intersections with emergency vehicles. A BMW had gone through a signal knocked out by the power failure and smacked into a Volvo, spreading bits of both vehicles everywhere. The fifteen minute drive from Darlene's had somehow more than doubled.

But he was home now. It was Christmas Eve, he reminded himself. He needed to get on his Christmas cheer.

"Trey?" He heard a quick tap of heels and Olivia threw herself into his arms. "Thank God you're back," she said in a rush. "He's here."

"Who?"

"Bradley."

"Bradley? In the house?"

She shook her head. "Not here. Not now, anyway. He stopped by earlier. With a man. Someone foreign." She shuddered.

Skele, he thought.

"I tried to call you."

"There's a power outage. Cell service is knocked out." He felt her shaking, an ongoing tremor that she didn't seem able to suppress. "What did he say?" Lex asked urgently, drawing her over to a couch to sit. "Mom, come on, try to calm down. What happened?"

"He…he was different. I don't know, closed, hard. I begged him to turn himself in and he refused. He wanted something in Pierce's office."

The key, Lex thought immediately. "Did you go with him? What did he take?" He fought the urge to rush her, fought the urge to check for himself. She was holding on by one very thin thread. "Mom, did he take the key?"

"I don't…what key?"

Lex exhaled slowly and fought for calm. "It's really important that you tell me exactly what he said."

"He asked who'd been in the office. He seemed angry. I told him you'd been there. And Keely. Oh, she stopped by earlier. She said something about going to the house."

At the house alone, with Bradley. And Skele. "Jesus," he said.

"What's going on?"

He was on his feet before she finished the words. "Call the cops," he shouted, running to the door. "28 Candlewood Highway."

"Lex, *wait.* I can't call the police on him."

"*Do it,*" he snapped. "Tell them a woman's in danger there. Tell them what Bradley's done. Tell them to call Stockton. *Now.*" And he sprinted for his Jeep.

The wheels of the car crunched to a stop on the snowy driveway before the house. Keely turned off the engine, her sigh of relief sounding very loud in the sudden silence. It had taken over half an hour but she was here.

Somehow it didn't seem nearly as imperative as it had when she'd been comfortably curled up in her parents' house. Why hadn't she just waited for morning and daylight? What difference would another ten or twelve hours have made?

Darkness pressed in around the car. When she got out, the silence was almost oppressive, save for the faint ticks of the heavy, wet snowflakes hitting. Outside the car, she found the silence was almost oppressive. She was used to garages, streetlights, civilization. The emptiness all around her made her skin crawl.

The enormous black anodized flashlight her father had given her might have been big enough to double as a baseball bat, but the beam didn't seem to go very far in the woods. It was as though the acres of darkness sucked up every ray the flashlight emitted. Out in the darkness, a stick snapped and the hairs rose on the back of her neck. A raccoon, she told herself, or a cat, or some night critter that was probably just going about its bloodthirsty little life, unconcerned and unaware that it was scaring her silly.

She wrapped her jacket more tightly around herself and hurried to the side porch. The sooner she was inside, the better.

It was embarrassing to admit just how creepy it was to turn her back to the darkness long enough to unlock the door. And how creepy it was to walk into a black house. She'd definitely been out of her mind to come there alone, but she was too stubborn to admit she was chicken and run home. As soon as she stepped inside, she whirled to lock the door behind her, her heart thudding in her ears. What she needed was a few dozen spotlights or torches. What she had was the flashlight. It wasn't enough.

It was all she had.

In the end, she settled for standing it on end on the desk so that the beam shone up to the ceiling. The resultant illumination was dim but more or less even. Thank God Bradley had bought a laptop rather than a desktop system or she'd have been dead in the water. With the laptop battery, she'd have at least three or four hours to look around.

Assuming she was right about the password.

The laptop was new enough that it was WiFi ready, so she just turned on the antenna and let it find the network on its own, signing on with her parents' username and password. And then she was at the VoIP site. She could feel her heart beginning to thud a little faster. More than anything, she wished Lex were there with her.

With a few clicks of the keys, she typed in the two parts of the sign-on. "Okay, Bradley, come through for me," she muttered, and pressed Enter. For an endless moment, she just heard the sound of the pulse in her ears. Then the log-in screen disappeared.

She had entry to the files. Keely whooped without thinking, the sound eerie in the empty house. She felt as though she'd just gotten the key to the secret garden.

The list of voice mail messages went on and on. There were easily two dozen or more, several of them five or ten minutes in length, all of them no more than six months old. Intrigued, she clicked on one of them, turning the sound all the way up.

And Bradley's voice filled the room. "You have a routing number for the bank transfers?"

"Yes, of course. I can get you whatever you need." The speaker had a heavy Slavic accent; Skele, she was betting. The conversation centered around ways and means of transferring money from the coffers of a vendor corporation owned by Skele to Skele's own coffers.

It wasn't a voice mail message, it was a full-on conversation. Bradley had taped his phone calls and played those tapes to his voice mail, she realized. And they were safe. He didn't need a computer, didn't need a flash drive or audiotape. The VoIP company servers were keeping the files. If Bradley needed them, he could access them at any place and anytime, provided he had an Internet connection.

As leverage went, it was rather brilliant.

She worked her way through the messages on the list. Conversation after conversation contained damaging admissions by Skele. Midway down the list, she hit pay dirt. Again, it was Skele, speaking in his heavy, ponderous voice.

"I wish to be able to clean at least half of the money by the end of the year. I want more LLCs."

Bradley's response was unintelligible.

"Then you will make it convincing," Skele said in anoyance. "The board of directors, we need more American names."

"I don't have more names."

"Find some," Skele rumbled. "Use your mother, your girlfriend."

"They won't want any part of this."

"They will never know."

They will never know.

Relief made her weak. That was it, proof in Bradley and Skele's words that she and Olivia were innocent. In those few words, her entire life opened up.

Hands shaking, Keely dug through her purse for Stockton's card. Her cell phone was dead because of the power outage. E-mail would have to do. With a few keystrokes, she saved the voice mail message as an audio file and sent it to him in an e-mail.

The next message was older. This time, Skele and Bradley weren't such good buddies. This time, they were fighting. Skele, it appeared, wanted to scale up the operation. Bradley was getting cold feet.

"I have hundred million coming in next week from contact in Syria. I must wash money."

"I can't do it that quickly," Bradley said, "not unless you want to get caught."

And over the sound of the recording, she suddenly heard the door open.

She'd leapt to her feet and spun around before she even registered moving, to see Bradley—*Bradley*—standing in the gloom there.

"Why, Keely. What a surprise."

He looked different. Bulkier, maybe. Harder. There was something sinister about his face in the dim light. His eyes were shadowed.

And in his hand, he held a gun.

He wasn't alone. Skele, she thought with a shiver. It had to be. If ever she'd looked into the face of a killer, this had to be it. There was an unsettling, almost brutal sensuality to his features—fleshy lips, wide forehead, heavy jaw. Bradley held his gun like it was part of a costume he was trying on; Skele held it like it was an extension of his hand.

But it was his hooded eyes that made her skin crawl. The expression they held was worse than total indifference. It reminded her of the time she'd seen an alligator during a trip to Florida, a sense of looking into the eyes of some primordial consciousness that merely recognized her as moving, not alive.

"Bradley." She switched her gaze to him. "What are you doing here?"

Her heart hammered against her ribs as though it were trying to batter its way out. Her only choice was to keep them talking and see if she wound up with any chance for escape. To run through the frozen woods in the darkness, she thought forcing down the panic that pressed into her throat. Good luck.

"What am I doing here? Well, it's Christmas." Bradley stepped into the room, followed by Skele. "Doesn't everybody come home for the holidays? I've got a good reason to be here. You, on the other hand, are a whole different matter." His eyes hardened.

"It's my house, last time I checked," she said.

He blinked. "You've been a busy girl, I see." He'd drawn near enough to see what she was doing, to hear the conversation playing.

"You didn't leave me with a choice."

"Do you like the house? I just couldn't think what to get you as a wedding present," he said. "Then again, we're not getting married, are we?"

She stared at him, wondering how she'd ever thought she loved him. "I guess that depends on you," she said, surprised at how steady her voice sounded. "Going with you could be the best thing. After all, if I stick around, I'm probably looking at jail time, or so they tell me. As is your mother."

He flicked her a dismissive glance, where she stood beside the computer. "With all her money, she'll get off."

"Yes, well, all her money. That's an interesting question. They're talking about confiscating a large part of it because of the money you funneled through her account."

Out of the corner of her eye, she saw Skele whip his head around to stare at Bradley.

"What money?" His voice was silky.

"Nothing. It's of no concern to you," Bradley said.

"I have twenty-five million dollars in frozen accounts because of you. It is of great concern to me."

Slowly, an infinitesimal fraction at a time, Keely slid her hand out toward the flashlight that still stood upended on the desk. The darkness was her friend.

"The money she's talking about is not your money," Bradley said.

"It is all my money." Skele moved closer to the computer, his mouth hardening. She'd been wrong when she'd thought his eyes held only a primordial expression. They could also hold malice. "And what is this?" He gestured to the screen. "That is my voice, and yours, talking of business."

"Business records," Bradley blurted, swallowing.

"These business records, they have only one purpose." Skele stared at Bradley, then down at the screen, a vein on his temple pulsing.

Keely's hand crept nearer to the flashlight. Skele and

Bradley were completely focused on each other, turned half away from her. She could hear the blood rushing in her ears. One chance, she thought, stretching her fingers. She would have one chance only.

"Vilis, don't get excited." Bradley's voice sounded too loud, too hearty. "That's why we came here, to dust the computer and get rid of loose ends, right?"

"Yes, we get rid of loose ends." He raised the gun.

And Keely swung the heavy flashlight with all her might into the back of his head. The impact reverberated through her fingers, jarring the flashlight loose. Skele dropped like a stone.

Bradley swung around to her in shock, the gun leveled at her heart.

Keely swallowed. "Bradley," she said.

He retrieved the flashlight and studied Skele's prone body. "I suppose I should say thank you. I honestly think he meant to kill me." He sounded surprised.

He didn't shift the gun.

"He's had practice killing people, I understand. You should be more careful who you choose to do business with."

His brows lowered. "You shouldn't be here. If you hadn't been, everything would have been fine. You always were too smart for your own good."

It took her two tries to speak. "It won't do you any good to kill me. They already have an airtight case."

"Not without the laptop. And you. You heard Skele. No loose ends." Shadows hooded his eyes.

"Bradley, don't do this," she whispered.

"I have to," he said, almost pleading. "No loose ends." He thumbed off the safety.

There was a sound and Lex burst through the door, grabbing at Bradley's arm. A deafening explosion filled the room. Plaster showered down from where the bullet had entered the ceiling. The revolver skittered away.

Keely watched in horror as the two brothers grappled on the floor in the dimness, rolling over, knocking into Skele's unconscious form, fighting to get to the gun. "Stop it," she shouted, grabbing at the flashlight where it fallen, frantically trying to figure out a way to end the nightmare. And then she saw it—the gleam of metal by Skele's hand.

"Stop." She snatched the gun from the floor. "*Now.*" With shaking hands, she cocked the weapon.

The sharp click had the two men on the floor freezing, their heads whipping around to stare at her.

"Enough, Bradley. It's over." Her voice strenghtened. "It's over," she repeated as sirens sounded in the distance.

There were moments in life, Keely thought as she and Lex walked out of the police station, that you knew you'd never forget. Bradley pulling the gun, Lex leaping through the door. And yet, somehow, even in that moment, with Christmas morning dawning, the whole thing was impossible to believe. Less than twelve hours before, two men had held guns on her. Now, in houses all around them, children were wakening to the magic of presents and Santa Claus.

Bradley and Skele had been taken to the hospital, the laptop confiscated by Stockton for review. Stockton and his colleagues had questioned Keely and Lex all night. They'd been scolded, thanked, congratulated, exonerated.

And now they were outside, finally with a moment to themselves.

After everything that had happened, all that had passed between them, she hadn't a clue what to say. He had broken her heart and quite probably saved her life. He had saved her life and he was going to disappear into the sunset and she'd more than likely never see him again.

She couldn't bear it.

She stopped and swung around to look at him. Their breath came out in plumes of white in the chill air. "Thank you doesn't seem like enough, but it's all I have," she said. "You were wonderful."

"I should thank you. You were the one who stopped it."

"We both did."

"We're a hell of a team."

"We were," she said, fighting to keep her voice steady. "Thank you. I owe you my life." She leaned in to kiss his cheek.

And he grabbed her and pulled her to him convulsively, so that she almost couldn't breathe.

"I'm an idiot," Lex said savagely.

Keely blinked. "What?"

"I'm a pinhead. I so screwed up. I could have lost you. I love you and I could have lost you."

She stared at him, stunned. "What do you mean?" she asked faintly.

"Oh, God, Keely, I was out of my mind tonight when I was driving over there, knowing about Bradley and Skele, knowing that you were in danger. I was so wrong last week. I got scared," he said simply. "I've been on my own so long that I just couldn't deal with what was happening.

"And then tonight when I realized all of a sudden I might lose you, I found out what it was like to be really scared." He shook his head. "It's no good without you. I realized that. If you're not with me, whatever else there is, it just doesn't matter."

He swallowed and took her hand in his. "I love you, Keely. That was what you saw in my face the night of the gala. I was just too dense to realize it. I want to make this work."

And she laughed and threw her arms around him. "Oh, do you mean it?"

"I've never been more sure of anything in my life."

He was strong and solid and there and she'd never known what it was to feel happy before this moment. But they had to do it right. She leaned back and looked into his eyes. "I meant what I said last week, Lex. I love you but I don't want to trap you. I don't want this to be about you giving up something so we can be together. It can't work that way."

"I've got a chance to take a job in New York for a year, running the photo desk of the wire service. That gives us a good, solid start together."

"Don't give up what you love. It's too important, too much a part of you. We'll figure something out." She gave him a grin. "I might look cute in a burka, you never know."

"The thing is, I'd already about decided to take the job before this happened. The kind of assignments I take can grind you into dust if you don't watch it. I've been needing a break."

"Yeah, but this much of a break?" She held on to him, still unable to believe it.

"The year off will be good. After that, we'll see. I can still take assignments, I can still go out but I'll have a place to come back to. Wherever you are." He kissed her forehead. "We'll find a way to make it work. Maybe I'll decide I like it here."

"Here in New York or here, here?"

"What do you mean?

"I realized something, too, last night. I'm leaving New York." Ignoring his shock, she went on. "I want to come back here to live, start my own accounting business. I've already got Darlene as a client and she says she can get me more. And…well, you'll think it's silly…"

"What?"

"The safe house," she blurted out in a rush. "It's so gorgeous out there. When the case is over, it'll probably be up for auction. I was thinking about buying it."

"You want to buy a place where my brother held a gun on you?" He half laughed.

"I want to buy the place that we first made love. I mean, we might need to do some kind of a psychic cleansing on it, get rid of all the bad vibes."

He pulled her close to him. "I know just the way to do that. It's an ancient African ceremony that involves getting naked together, lots, in every room of the house."

"Well, if we're going to do it, we'll need to practice."

He grinned down at her. "Well, what are we waiting for? It's Christmas morning. Time to open your presents."

"My present is you."

When Kimberley Blackstone's father is
presumed dead, Kimberley is required to take
over the helm of Blackstone Diamonds. She
has to work closely with her ex, Ric Perrini, to
battle not only the press, but also the fierce
attraction still sizzling between them. Does Ric
feel the same...or is it the power her share of
Blackstone Diamonds will provide him as he
battles for boardroom supremacy.

Look for

VOWS &
A VENGEFUL GROOM
by
BRONWYN
JAMESON

Available January wherever you buy books

To fulfill his father's dying wish,
Greek tycoon Christos Niarchos must
marry Ava Monroe, a woman who
betrayed him years ago. But his soon-to-
be-wife has a secret that could rock
more than his passion for her.

Look for

THE GREEK
TYCOON'S
SECRET HEIR

by

KATHERINE
GARBERA

Available January wherever you buy books

REQUEST YOUR FREE BOOKS!
2 FREE NOVELS PLUS 2 FREE GIFTS!

SPECIAL EDITION®
Life, Love and Family!

YES! Please send me 2 FREE Silhouette Special Edition® novels and my 2 FREE gifts. After receiving them, if I don't wish to receive any more books, I can return the shipping statement marked "cancel." If I don't cancel, I will receive 6 brand-new novels every month and be billed just $4.24 per book in the U.S., or $4.99 per book in Canada, plus 25¢ shipping and handling per book and applicable taxes, if any*. That's a savings of at least 15% off the cover price! I understand that accepting the 2 free books and gifts places me under no obligation to buy anything. I can always return a shipment and cancel at any time. Even if I never buy another book from Silhouette, the two free books and gifts are mine to keep forever.

235 SDN EEYU   335 SDN EEY6

Name	(PLEASE PRINT)	
Address		Apt.
City	State/Prov.	Zip/Postal Code

Signature (if under 18, a parent or guardian must sign)

Mail to the **Silhouette Reader Service™**:
IN U.S.A.: P.O. Box 1867, Buffalo, NY 14240-1867
IN CANADA: P.O. Box 609, Fort Erie, Ontario L2A 5X3

Not valid to current Silhouette Special Edition subscribers.

Want to try two free books from another line?
Call 1-800-873-8635 or visit www.morefreebooks.com.

* Terms and prices subject to change without notice. NY residents add applicable sales tax. Canadian residents will be charged applicable provincial taxes and GST. This offer is limited to one order per household. All orders subject to approval. Credit or debit balances in a customer's account(s) may be offset by any other outstanding balance owed by or to the customer. Please allow 4 to 6 weeks for delivery.

Your Privacy: Silhouette is committed to protecting your privacy. Our Privacy Policy is available online at www.eHarlequin.com or upon request from the Reader Service. From time to time we make our lists of customers available to reputable firms who may have a product or service of interest to you. If you would prefer we not share your name and address, please check here. ☐

SSE07

Inside ROMANCE

Stay up-to-date on all your romance reading news!

Inside Romance is a FREE quarterly newsletter highlighting our upcoming series releases and promotions.

Visit

www.eHarlequin.com/InsideRomance

to sign up to receive our complimentary newsletter today!

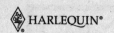

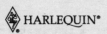

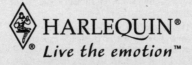

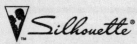
Silhouette®

COMING NEXT MONTH

SPECIAL EDITION

#1873 FALLING FOR THE M.D.—Marie Ferrarella
The Wilder Family
When Walnut River General Hospital received a takeover offer
from a large corporation, Dr. Peter Wilder butted heads with board
member Bethany Holloway, a staunch supporter of the merger. But
soon Peter realized he had a takeover target of his own: Bethany's
heart.

#1874 HIS SECOND-CHANCE FAMILY—RaeAnne Thayne
The Women of Brambleberry House
Returning to her seaside hometown was hard on widowed fifth-
grade teacher Julia Blair. But then she saw the For Rent sign on the
rambling Victorian and knew she and her twins had found home. Of
course, it helped when she realized the workman in the backyard was
Will Garrett, her childhood sweetheart all grown up....

#1875 THE BILLIONAIRE AND HIS BOSS—Patricia Kay
The Hunt for Cinderella
Philanthropist Alex Hunt needed to find a bride within a year or
his wealthy father would disinherit him and jeopardize his charity
work. So, to avoid the gold diggers, Alex took a fake name and a
blue-collar job...and formed an instant attraction to his new boss
P. J. Kincaid. But was P.J. also pretending to be someone she wasn't?

#1876 YOURS, MINE...OR OURS?—Karen Templeton
Guys and Daughters
For ex-cop Rudy Vaccaro, buying a 150-year-old New Hampshire
inn was a dream come true. But his preteen daughter felt very
differently about the matter—as did Violet Kildare, the former
owner's maid, who'd been promised the property. Sympathetic, Rudy
let Violet keep her job...not knowing he was getting a new lease on
life and love in return.

#1877 YOU, AND NO OTHER—Lynda Sandoval
Return to Troublesome Gulch
Police officer Cagney Bishop had always lived in the shadow of
her bullying police chief father—especially when he ran her first
love Jonas Eberhardt out of town. Now Jonas was back, a wealthy
man, funding the local teen center to show that Troublesome Gulch
hadn't defeated him. But would Jonas's true gift be to offer Cagney a
second chance?

#1878 FOR JESSIE'S SAKE—Kate Welsh
Abby Hopewell felt betrayed by men—especially her only true love,
Colin McCarthy. When they were young, he'd callously left her in
the lurch and split town. Or so Abby thought. Now Colin was back,
his daughter, Jessie, in tow, and Abby's bed-and-breakfast was the
only place to stay. It was time to revisit the past....

SSECNM1207